SAD BASTARD

Hugo Hamilton was born in Dublin of Irish-German parentage. He was brought up with three languages: Irish, German and English, and educated in Irish-language schools. He has published three highly acclaimed novels set in Germany, the collection of short stories *Dublin Where the Palm Trees Grow*, and most recently the novel *Headbanger*. He has recently spent some time as writer-in-residence in Bucharest and York. He lives and works in Dublin.

ALSO BY HUGO HAMILTON

Surrogate City
The Last Shot
The Love Test
Dublin Where the Palm Trees Grow
Headbanger

Hugo Hamilton

SAD BASTARD

VINTAGE

Published by Vintage 1999

2 4 6 8 10 9 7 5 3 1

Copyright © by Hugo Hamilton 1998

The right of Hugo Hamilton to be identified as the author
of this work has been asserted by him in accor-
dance with the Copyright, Designs and Patents Act, 1988

First published in Great Britain by
Secker & Warburg in 1998

Vintage
Random House, 20 Vauxhall Bridge Road,
London SW1V 2SA

Random House Australia (Pty) Limited
20 Alfred Street, Milsons Point, Sydney
New South Wales 2061, Australia

Random House New Zealand Limited
18 Poland Road, Glenfield,
Auckland 10, New Zealand

Random House South Africa (Pty) Limited
Endulini, 5A Jubilee Road, Parktown 2193,
South Africa

Random House UK Limited Reg. No. 954009

A CIP catalogue record for this book
is available from the British Library

ISBN 0 09 927499 X

Papers used by Random House UK Ltd are natural,
recyclable products made from wood grown in sustain-
able forests. The manufacturing processes conform to the
environmental regulations of the country of origin

Printed and bound in Great Britain by
Cox & Wyman Limited, Reading, Berkshire

For my sisters, Máire, Ita and Bríd

Coyne sat drinking his pint. Minding his own business. Like many other men alone at bar counters throughout the city of Dublin, he looked like he was driving something big. Sitting on a high stool, steering a crane, or a truck, or a bus full of half-drunk passengers. He was leaning forward a little and staring straight ahead at the inverted spirit bottles – Hussar, Paddy, Napoleon, Cork Dry. As always, his wheatfield hair was standing up on his head. As always, he looked like he'd just had an idea.

He called over the barman and ordered a gin and tonic.

Behind him in the background, there was a click of pool and the wash of voices from the back bar. The TV was like a grotto in the top corner with the faithful flock staring up in blind devotion. Traffic rocked the bar as it passed by outside. And from the lounge next door, the nasal lament of a band howling through bathroom acoustics: *You don't know what it's like.* Dragging through the words, like red fingernails down along the spine.

What on earth did Pat Coyne think he was up to? Gin and tonic was not his kind of drink. It was an odd decision all right, and the barman did a quick double-check with his eyes, announcing the name of the drink in bold to make sure he hadn't got it wrong before he mechanically dropped ice and lemon into a glass, pushed it under the Cork Dry teat and sent clear air bubbles floating up through the bottle. Turned and whisked the cap from the tonic.

Coyne nodded. The symbolic gin and tonic sitting beside his solitary pint. It was for Carmel. Coyne's estranged wife,

I

Carmel. Some distant hope that she would walk into the Anchor Bar and sit down beside him.

As always, Coyne was talking to himself. Explaining every move he made. Justifying his contorted logic to the inner audience in his head. If somebody was to draw a map of Coyne's mind, some kind of three-dimensional elevation of his intellect, it would look something like the Burren landscape of County Clare – full of shale and fissures and layered escarpments, full of complicated underground channels of water and all kinds of exotic plant life surviving in the most unlikely places. In matters of the head, this temporarily off-duty, perhaps soon to be ex-Garda, was an enigma even to himself at times. Damaged, some might say.

The Anchor Bar was full of familiar faces. Some of the ferry workers were playing pool in the back. McCurtain from the Port and Docks board was there, talking his head off to some of the fishing people from the harbour, while in the snug as usual, the poet was sifting through a manuscript, mouthing words to himself. One of the barmen was acting as a kind of quiz master, asking some of the men how many airports there were in Ireland. Think about it, he said, and the men pondered over their pints, knowing that there had to be some kind of catch.

It was a quiet sort of place, with wooden compartments for separation and lots of nautical artefacts such as a copper beacon, Admiralty charts of the Irish Sea, pictures of Galway hookers and bottles of Finest Sea Dog rum that nobody ever drank. There was a brass clock and a brass bell which they rang in desperation at closing time as if they were on a sinking ship. After which all the drowning people would desert the vessel and stand outside on the pavement talking. It was the kind of place that left the Christmas decorations up all year long – a furry red, tinsel boa draped all around the top of the bar along with a set of fairy lights. It was a place for all types. A ferryport refuge at the back end of Dun Laoghaire. And Dun Laoghaire was the back door of Dublin city. And Ireland was the snug of Europe.

Coyne ordered a further gin and tonic. And later on another, even though he knew she wasn't coming. It made no sense. Would have been a true miracle. An apparition. Three untouched gins and three full bottles of tonic stood lined up on the bar counter alongside his own pint on the highly improbable, more than impossible odds that she might stride in through the door. Coyne even looked around from time to time whenever he heard the squeak of hinges. No chance. He was a sad bastard.

Coyne had been off work for five months now since the fire. Injured in the line of duty. His wounds had healed to a greater degree, but the acid lick of flames had left its marks, like embossed hieroglyphics on his back. His lungs too had suffered smoke damage, and water damage, like blackened walls and waterlogged carpets. Occasionally, he was forced to stop in the street to cough uncontrollably. Traffic coming to a halt as he rasped and dregged up some magnificent verdigris trophies. Jesus, some of the stuff Coyne had uncovered in his chest since the fire should have been exhibited.

But these were only minor problems in comparison to the subliminal damage. No amount of compensation could make up for the unquantifiable psychological scars. He was jumpy and unreasonable. Sometimes angry and uncontrollably moody. Potentially violent, even. Suffering from a range of emotional problems and currently undergoing a series of psychiatric assessments to determine whether he was fit for work. He was regularly attending a therapist, though with great reluctance. He didn't believe in that sort of thing.

Coyne was refusing to co-operate. He resented the interference and hated the sound of encouraging words.

3

Turned down all medication and mistrusted every prognosis. He would have preferred a good ending – the nobility of things coming to a close. He wanted to go out in glory. And this was perhaps the key to the hidden backlands of Coyne's unfathomable psyche. He didn't want to be healed.

Coyne – the man they could not cure. The code they could not break.

Tommy Nolan came into the Anchor Bar towards the end of the night. The last pub on his odyssey. He came in the back door and drifted around the bar greeting the regulars one by one. He was everybody's friend. Did odd jobs for people at the harbour, like a grown-up child or an orphan that everybody took under their wing; a harmless, good-willed man with a limp and a stammer who still lived with his older sister Marlene in a small corporation flat nearby.

Coyne bought him a pint.

I have to tell you something, Tommy said.

Tommy sometimes repaid the pints with bits of information. He had a serious speech impediment, with saliva spilling from his mouth, like a tap that could not be fully switched off. Lips soft and glistening.

Coyne looked up and tried to read Tommy's lips. Then watched him opening his mouth wide to drink from his pint. Black liquid sloshing back and forth between the glass and his mouth. An exchange of fluids in which it was hard to establish if there was more of it rushing in or more saliva rushing back out, until the whole lot finally drained down and Tommy Nolan smiled at Coyne with his red face, and a brown dribble running down from the corner of his mouth. Ready to start the next pint.

The *Lolita*, Tommy spluttered.

He was showering Coyne with a spray of diluted Guinness and local gossip. Hosing down the whole place with droplet infection, trying to tell Coyne about the illegal imports. Right here at the harbour. The *Lolita* had just come in an hour ago. No cargo of fish. No ice-boxes. No trailing flag of seagulls.

Coyne looked around uneasily. Not here, he thought, putting up his hand. He didn't want people to think that Tommy was a scout or an informer of some kind. Once a cop always a cop in the eyes of the public at large.

Besides, Coyne was preoccupied by his own internal world these days. He had no real interest in crime any more. He was looking for broader solutions, something more global than the ordinary day-to-day activity around this coastal suburb of Dublin.

By then they had started ringing the bell and the Anchor Bar was going down fast. The band next door had finished at last with an almighty crescendo that went on like a five-minute orgasm at the end of every night. End after end, amen. McCurtain from the Port and Docks board was furtively receiving a no-cover, porn video from one of the ferry workers. And Coyne was still sitting at the bar with his three gin and tonics in front of him, beaming out like beacons of love and betrayal. He might as well have been looking at the emptiness of the Irish Sea by night. Lines of latitude; streaks of foam; wave after wave rolling unrelentingly towards him across the wide open counter on a black night. Another lonely bell clanging furiously next door and men shouting 'time'.

He began to pour the tonics into the gins. Then shared the lot into two equal glasses, and handed one over to Tommy.

Here you are, Tommy. Knock it back.

Put it this way, it was a waste of time trying to bring Coyne back to normal. He had never been normal in the first place, and was hardly going to fit into the parameters of textbook sanity at this point. His psychologist, Ms Clare Dunford kept encouraging him to try and put the past behind him and to seek personal satisfaction. Not to feel so guilty about peace and pleasure. She talked about happiness as if it was the ultimate goal. As though everybody had a moral duty to be content and make the most of life. And nobody was ever allowed to be sad, or unfulfilled, or maladjusted ever again.

Coyne's ex-wife, Carmel was the same, trying to arrange appointments for Coyne to go to all kinds of healers and alternative practitioners. Even though they had been separated for over a year now and Coyne was exiled from the family home in his own two-roomed flat, she was still devoted to fixing him up. He presented a real challenge. Anyone who met Coyne thought to themselves – I could repair him. Christ, that man needs help. He should be on medication. But Coyne had developed the protective coat of a hedgehog, balling himself up into an untouchable mass against the society around him, with a shield of cynicism and indifference. He had become a solitary creature. A dissident on the Happy Block.

Don't take away my pain, is what he bawled at his psychologist on the first encounter, when she spoke about the properties of Prozac.

I mean, what else would a man have to hold on to. If he was cured and normal, then he was as good as dead. They would take away his roar and leave him like a defenceless creature. A certain amount of chaos and insanity was vital to his existence. Rage and insanity were national characteristics. There was mayhem and derangement in his blood, which couldn't be erased that simply without turning Coyne into some kind of benevolent Frankenstein.

Coyne had been told already on numerous occasions that he had a fixation with the past. He was unable to move forward. The clock had stopped with the symmetry of a significant ending, somewhere around 5:55. The calendar hadn't moved on since the day of the fire and he was holding on to history. He had no current story for his life except the old one. I only listen to songs that evoke

6

memories, he revealed under psychoanalysis. He kept getting into arguments, and generally behaving badly, complaining about things that nobody took seriously but him. Unfit for work. Unfit for society.

The Anchor Bar was closed. Barstools placed upside down on the counter. The barman was sweeping the cigarette butts into a corner and the lounge next door was silent and empty, except for the musicians packing up their gear. The pool table at the back was in darkness and the bar was deserted, with a high blue cloud of smoke and conversation still hanging in the air. Somebody counting the till.

Coyne was the last to leave. He went home along the seafront, feeling the breeze blowing in off the sea. He saw the black water of the harbour and the row of trawlers berthed along the quay. He saw the sleazy, orange-pink glow coming across the water from the city. The yellow lights of Dublin Bay lit up like a tinted crystal bowl. The twin stacks of the Pigeon House with its red beacon lights and the flag of dusty-pink smoke drifting inland.

He walked home along streets of B&Bs and guesthouses. Past all the names like Stella Maris and Belleview. Santander or Casablanca. With tacky palm trees outside casting a subtropical illusion, and leatherette leaves whispering on the breeze. Gardens with stones and rocks pillaged from the coast and placed in neat decorative lines on the edges of grass lawns; around flowerbeds and benches. Suburbia's last line of defence. The whole borough had barricaded itself in behind these stones. Streets named Tivoli, Adelaide and Villarea. Maretimo Terrace. Sefton and Grafton. Houses that sounded like they came from a shaggin' Yeats poem, like Ben Bulben, Lissadel. Where did these people think they were? Where was Phil Lynott Avenue?

Coyne lived on Crosthwaite Park, or Cross-eyed Park as they called it. This was the flat where he had spent the past

7

twelve months or so with his son, Jimmy. These were the separation terms – Coyne looked after Jimmy, while Carmel kept home and looked after Jennifer and Nuala. It was not a final, end of all communication, separation, and there were still a lot of common areas of concern that allowed the marriage to linger on at a distance.

Coyne still talked to Carmel in his head.

It's not the way you think, he said, indirectly giving her a report on his life as he climbed the stairs and entered his flat. She was the inner audience to whom he offered his querulous commentary.

Look, the place is tidy, he pleaded. It's not a health hazard, you know. Look at the tea-towel neatly hung up on the stove. Look at the crockery all washed and put away. I know I'm a useless cook, but I do my best. I look after him, Carmel. I swear! Jimmy's a good lad.

But there was something reductive about this one-way conversation. He sat down in despair, as though people had stopped listening to him. His audience had gone to sleep again. He watched a *National Geographic* video on spiders. A male spider was plucking the web of a female. Serenading spiders! Web harpists! Would Coyne ever be reunited with Carmel? seemed to be the question all nature was asking.

Coyne woke up in his armchair some time later, stiff and numb along his left arm. He got up and switched off the TV, went over to the phone and dialled a number. He waited a while until the phone was picked up at the other end and a sleepy male voice answered. It was the voice of his old bank manager, Mr Killmurphy.

Hello, Killjoy, Coyne said.

The voice on the other end was stunned. Hello! Hello! Who is this?

Remember the patio, Killjoy. Remember the bitumen all over your crazy paving. And the granite barbecue in the shape of a miniature Norman castle. Remember the garden terrorist.

Who is this?

I'm coming back Killjoy. I hope you haven't forgotten, you bastard.

I'm going to call the Guards!

The phone went dead and Coyne smiled. This was part of a new campaign of remembrance. What was the point in letting Mr Killmurphy walk away from the past? Coyne was playing the role of civic conscience here, meting out punishment and retribution to an old enemy. Coyne, the sad bastard, standing by the phone with the grin of a sick deviant on his face, carrying the mother of all grudges in his heart.

Coyne's son, Jimmy was pissed out of his head that night. Rat arsed! Maybe even off his face on some other substances. How Coyne had missed running into him was remarkable. They practically crossed each other's paths as Jimmy and his friend Gussy made their way towards the harbour. His son was a headbanger, following in his father's footsteps. Except that Jimmy had no declared idealism other than getting out of his head.

He was insane in the membrane, as the song went, with little sense of self-respect. He and Gussy were on their way to do damage. They had their minds fixed on getting into one of the yachts on the marina.

They were not looking for anything in particular. It was more like a general quest for the crack. A bit of harmless sport. Or maybe Jimmy had lost it, somehow, since Coyne and Carmel broke up. Perhaps he was the real victim, acting out the fracture of his parents' marriage in a more dramatic form, for all to see. He and Gussy made their way on to a yacht and kicked in the cabin door. Opened the fridge and found it stocked with champagne and sausages. Started celebrating right away so that Jimmy got twice as drunk again and couldn't even stand up. Sat on a mound of sausages and laughed uncontrollably as he opened up a tube of Pringles.

Once you start, you can't stop, he said, as it rained Pringles all over the cabin floor.

Jimmy didn't even have the sense to leave the flare gun alone. While the champagne corks were popping and Gus started spraying the stuff around like a rally winner, Jimmy struck back with a flare which suddenly ripped through the cabin like a red meteor. Almost took Gussy's face off and sent him back, dribbling champagne over himself in shock while the flare continued to spin and fizzle around on the floor, burning a crest in the navy carpet. Big black Cyrillic script. The whole cabin lit up pink like a love boat. Pink portholes throbbing until Gus covered it with a jacket and snuffed out the brief comet's life.

How they weren't spotted by the harbour police was a miracle.

Jesus Christ, Gussy said, and within minutes they were back on the pier again. Jimmy getting sick into an empty Pringles tin, as though it had been specially provided for seasickness. Hanging over the blue railings like a puking pilgrim, retching up his ancestors.

Gussy made a run for it. But Jimmy didn't see the point. He found himself a sheltered place along the pier and sat down. Watched the swell of the tide lapping against the steps in the harbour. Tried to focus on the swirling red beam of the lighthouse for a while until he laid his head down on the cool granite stone and fell asleep. The sea was calm. A heron stood on the steps close by, like a silent witness.

Around that time, two men were driving along the coast road towards the harbour in a red van. The man at the wheel was the skipper of the *Lolita*, a chubby, forty-year-old man by the name of Martin Davis. Bald with a full-blown, bushy brown beard, he carried an extensive bit of freight out front, like a beanbag paunch hanging over the belt of his trousers. He was convinced that women liked a big belly with soft black fleece. It could be massaged and slapped. A convex sign of prosperity, fun and formidable appetite.

In the passenger seat, with his legs stretched out, sat a wiry man by the name of Mongi O Doherty who interpreted the bulging shape of the skipper's stomach as a sign of weakness. The exploitable, soft underbelly of a man devoted to pleasure.

Mongi was younger than the skipper, with a shaven head and a different temperament entirely. He saw pleasure as something you stole from others. He had been brought up in an environment where pleasure was something you grabbed while you had the chance, something that was normally associated with another person experiencing pain and dispossession.

As everyone knew, pain and pleasure were the same thing, only on opposite ends of the scale. Understanding this was the basis of capitalism; if you didn't grasp the barometer of human longing, then you were fucked as far as making money was concerned. At the point of a knife, or a dirty needle, it was surprising, for example, how quickly people despised their own material belongings. Moneylending and drug sales had also proved this point beyond any doubt. And a gun, well that was the true revolution. At the point of a gun, you had people begging you to take their money. Fear and pain altered everything.

With these elementary rules of commerce, Mongi had developed true leadership qualities.

The name Mongi had various sources. One of them is thought to have had something to do with his protruding teeth. People recognized an uncomfortable combination of the benign Bee Gees smile and a savage horse-bite of yellow neglect. His smile was a kuru grin of cannibal revenge, and his laughter produced a kind of echo over the city of

Dublin. The hollow laugh! The millennial laugh of progress. The great capitalist laugh of eternal growth and incessant innovation.

It was rumoured that Mongi had once bitten a Garda in the face. Leading people to believe that the origins of his name had more to do with the style of the mongoose, darting in and out rapidly to bite its prey. But the irony only fully ripened when you discovered that his nickname Mongi actually came from the word *mangach* in the Irish language, meaning toothless. His real name was Richard O Doherty.

To hell with fishing, he was saying to his new associate, Martin Davis. Fishing had become an extinguished way of life belonging to the last century.

You're dead right, skipper Martin Davis agreed.

Everywhere around the Irish coast had been fished to bejaysus. Mackerel-crowded seas, my arse. You had to compete with a massive fleet. Every factory ship in Europe was out there grabbing the same statistical slice of fish pie, fighting like a bunch of cut-throat pirates over the Atlantic fish-finger quota. Nobody would eat the glow-in-the-dark radioactive plaice from the Irish Sea any more. And what was the point in braving all kinds of inclement conditions, getting your hands raw like the Man of Aran and risking your life for a bit of stinking turbot. Every piece of fresh cod was marked and numbered on a radar screen; caught, gang-raped, cooked and consumed before you had a chance to slip the mooring.

Fishing is a cold and smelly business, Mongi said gravely.

Don't be talking, Martin Davis said, a grimace of disgust on his face.

You probably spent more money on fucking talcum powder than you earned on the catch.

Old Spice!

The skipper couldn't agree more. He was nodding like a rear-window travel dog. I hate the fish trade, he was saying. I hate all those biblical innuendoes. Casting out nets.

Gathering souls and all that stuff. Look, Mongi – I know what you're saying here. I've seen the movie.

But Mongi continued to place his own philosophical spin on the new dawn of opportunity. He was putting forward a vision for his people. The Irish were through with subsistence economics. He was the right man to be talking, with a name like Mongi. As they sped towards the harbour in the skipper's new van, he sounded like a fishmonger, glorifying the new enterprise of loaves and fishes. Sudden abundance! Economic miracles! All that had changed was the nature of the catch.

Wet-backs!

Fish-backs!

Wet-backs and fish-backs, Mongi echoed with his hollow cackle.

They could see the lights of the harbour below them. Two piers reaching out into the sea, embracing the visitor. Grabbing trade from the outside world.

Can you believe it? Mongi said. People paying money to get into Ireland. Remember when all we ever did was send out emigrants through that harbour. Every story ended with a man or a woman taking the boat to England. Remember the sign on the old mail boat as you walked across the gangplank: *Mind Your Step!* The last word of advice to the Irish exile.

Who woulda thought? Skipper echoed.

That's the new frontier, Mongi pointed, lighting up a cheroot in celebration.

If I woulda-hada known it was going to be like this, I woulda-never-hada busted my balls on the fishing for so long, the skipper said.

Fucking frontier is what I'm saying.

Mongi liked to repeat catchphrases to great literary effect. It gave things profundity. Added a cheap metaphysical lacquer to his words. Made him an innovator. He liked to remind people that there was such a thing as original thought, and it came from him. Out there in the future, the face of Mongi O Doherty would some day appear on the Ecu banknote.

Without me, you'd be nowhere, captain.

Martin Davis kept his humble mouth shut; just nodded in compliance. They had gone through all of this before. But since there was so much money involved, perhaps it was necessary to define the roles again. Who was the boss, in other words. Who was the creative genius behind this new enterprise.

Without me and my European connections, you'd still have fish scales on your mickey, Mongi continued. Without me, you'd be out there near Rockall with a floppy herring in your hand, like some prehistoric islandman. Spanking the mackerel! Jesus, Mongi laughed. No wonder people in Ireland hate fish.

Bud asail, the skipper muttered in Gaelic through his beard. The peasant revenge.

Mongi's grasp of the Irish language wasn't so hot. But he knew enough to understand that the word *bud* referred to the male prosthetic supplement. Mickey. Mackerel. He looked around angrily, demanding to know what the skipper was unhappy about. He had left fishing behind and was making serious money. All he had to do was bring in a consignment of illegal immigrants, hand over the money to Mongi, take his share and then go and get bricked out of his head. Eat food, get drunk and get laid for a few weeks until the next lot was to be brought in.

It was the new frontier all right. The *Lolita* rose and fell gently on the tide, with its human cargo of East Europeans still below deck, waiting to disembark. They were stiff from sitting on the cramped bunks of the two small cabins, looking out through a porthole at the bilge pump gushing rhythmically through the side of the next boat. Some of them were pale with seasickness and still vomiting into

14

plastic bags. They couldn't wait to see Ireland. They had paid good money to get this far.

The journey was not over yet, though, and according to plan they would have to spend some more time in the back of the van, until the skipper saw fit to release them on to the streets of the capital. Drop them at some labour exchange. Or just show them where to get the 46A into town.

The van reversed along the quay and the men got out. Martin Davis did what all truck drivers and van drivers do at this point; he adjusted his trousers and put everything back in place. He hopped out of the cab, stood with his legs apart and briefly performed that obligatory freedom jiggle, giving his trousers a little shake and pulling them up over his hips again before moving on. Then he followed Mongi and stepped on board the *Lolita* like an immigration officer.

For Jesus sake, Mongi hissed through his horse-teeth as he heard the singing below deck. The immigrants had been in those cabins too long and were trying to keep their spirits up, dancing and singing to combat poverty and loneliness and homesickness.

They're as bad as the Irish, Mongi roared. Can't go anywhere without starting a party. Drinking plum brandy and enjoying themselves. Singing sad songs.

Martin Davis hammered his fist on the door of the cabin and everything fell silent. Then he rooted under a seat and handed Mongi a red sportsbag.

Jesus, man. I said Irish or sterling!

What could I do? the skipper pleaded. I could hardly send them back.

What am I supposed to do with this stuff? Mongi held up a bundle of dollars, threw it back into the bag and zipped it up. It's awkward.

What was far more awkward was the presence of Tommy Nolan on the pier. He was on to this reverse emigration business. Already he had witnessed one consignment arriving a few weeks back. He had gone to the harbour after the pub and concealed himself on the quay, behind a stack of fish boxes and a mound of damaged blue nets. Behind him some tyres and ropes to sit on; and the smell of diesel and paint and piss all round. The lighting was poor and some of the lamps on the pier were missing. Tommy kept his eye on the trawlers shifting on the tide. Listening to the wood squeaking and groaning, so that he nearly fell asleep himself.

Until he saw the van arriving and the men getting out. Exhaust fumes drifting towards him.

After a while, Mongi came up on deck again carrying the holdall bag. Stepped off the boat and threw the bag into the front of the van and shut the door again. He stood around, smoking. The smell of cigar smoke blending with the smell of exhaust as he began to pace up and down beside the van.

Fuck this, Mongi muttered impatiently and jumped back on to the boat, down below to speed up the immigration procedure. He was demanding expediency that nobody could ever get used to. His people had been brought up on a spiritual sense of hope that ran counter to crass, wash-and-go, Euro-efficiency. They had lived on the imagination for so long that they didn't know how to grasp the material urgency of the moment. They still thrived on the accident, the casual diversion, the gift of surprise. The twist out of nowhere!

At this precise moment, Jimmy Coyne walked down the quay. Refreshed from his sleep, he walked straight towards the red van as though he had just parked it there himself. His face was disfigured with the imprint of granite on his cheek. His mind was disfigured with drink and sleep. But he seemed to walk straight with a great air of purpose. Assumed that the new van on the pier had been placed there for him, with the engine running and all.

People were driving all kinds of new vehicles in Dublin these days. He opened the door of the cab and got in.

Didn't even notice the holdall bag on the passenger seat and just started playing with the clutch and grinning to himself like a half-wit, getting ready to drive away when the door opened.

Beside him on the pier stood Tommy Nolan, mouthing at him like a guardian angel, begging him to stop. This is unconstitutional, he was trying to point out, with saliva streaming from his mouth. Trouble is close behind. Think about this – get out and walk away slowly before it becomes irreversible.

Jimmy pushed Tommy away. Slammed the door and got ready to drive.

In the meantime, Mongi had come up on deck with Martin Davis behind him. The immigrants with their bags down below at the bottom of the steps, eagerly waiting to be told to come up and breathe the misty night air. Mongi leaped on to the pier in disbelief and grabbed Tommy Nolan by the neck.

You dirtbird bastard! Mongi shouted, dragging him over to the edge of the pier. I fucking warned you.

Jimmy Coyne considered hiding, or escaping out the far door of the van. He looked out and saw Mongi turning around. Made eye contact with him, just before the van leaped forward with a terrible gear-grinding sound of agony.

Mongi was left standing on the pier, looking into the harbour. Then he tried to run after the van, tripping over a rusted brown mooring ring as he went. But Jimmy had managed to put the van in second gear and was already driving away up the hill towards the main road.

This was Black Monday for Mongi O Doherty. This was share freefall. He looked into the harbour and then back up to the main road where the van now disappeared. Nothing on the pain/pleasure scale was more agonizing than being ripped off due to your own carelessness. This was like biting your own tongue. This was like catching your foreskin in the zip. Like mistaking your own mickey for a mackerel.

Coyne made another phone call before he went to bed that night. It was something that had to be done with systematic dedication. Some things could not be dropped and forgotten. No way! Terrorism was an exact science that had to be consistent, unrelenting.

Killjoy, there is something I have to tell you, Coyne said into the phone as soon as it was answered.

If you don't stop this I'll call the Guards! I'll get this call traced.

Killjoy, you stupid bastard. You intransigent fucking moron. I hope that taught you a lesson. You'll live to regret the day. Killjoy, I hope they give you a pig's heart.

Tommy Nolan's body had no obvious marks when it was taken from the water the following morning. There was a lot of activity around the harbour, with blue lights flashing across the side of yachts and reflected in portholes. A sense of shock had already spread through the borough. Shopkeepers were talking. People stopped their cars along the main road overlooking the seafront. A crowd had gathered behind the yellow crime scene tape, looking down into the harbour. Into the gap between the trawlers and the pier where the debris normally collected into a compilation of styrofoam boxes, plastic litre bottles of Bulmers and Sprite, bits of saturated wood and usually a condom, floating in a greasy film of rainbow coloured diesel.

Tommy's body was discovered by one of the fishermen. The skipper of the *Lolita*, Martin Davis. Sergeant Corrigan from the local Garda station took a statement. Apart from some rope burn marks around Tommy's chest and a single bruise on the head which might also have occurred when he fell into the water, there was nothing to indicate foul play as such. These marks could have been consistent with a fall across the mooring ropes, and while the state pathologist was still going through his examination, the whole thing was explained as a tragedy. Gardai were of the opinion that Tommy Nolan might have been knocked unconscious by a fall against the hull of a boat after which he had become entangled in the mooring ropes. They were keeping an open mind – waiting for witnesses to come forward.

Coyne was down at the harbour himself that morning. As it happened, he was half keeping an eye out for Tommy Nolan and only became aware of his death some time later. Coyne was wandering around the area as though his life was one big Bloomsday, getting in touch with the real world, discovering all the extraneous, non-essential details he had been deprived of while working with the Gardai. Like water slapping against the steps. The echoes of the harbour. The sheen of sunlight on the surface of the water and the sound of bells everywhere, warped on the breeze. Coiling like oval rings across the tide.

He saw Garda activity on the far side of the harbour and went over. Stood on the edge of the crowd and finally heard the news. He started blaming himself immediately, spiralling into another bout of guilt and self-effacing torment. He should have listened to Tommy while he had the chance. He had failed him. A further instance of Coyne's inability to deal with the world.

Jimmy Coyne and Gus Mangan were arrested just before lunchtime.

Coyne received a call from Carmel in the early afternoon. There was a touch of bitterness in her voice that he had never heard before. A plaintive tone. As though all of this was Coyne's fault. As though he had instructed Jimmy to create havoc in order to provoke her. Coyne was doing all of this on purpose.

You better go down and straighten things out, she said. It was no surprise that Jimmy had ended up in some kind of trouble. He was starting to drift. And Coyne had no way of being firm with him. Jimmy often stayed out all night. The eldest son of a broken home, at liberty to come and go as he pleased. Whenever Coyne's atrocious cooking got too much for him, he went home for a meal in the family home with Carmel. Barely nineteen and in custody already.

Leave it to me, Coyne reassured her. He would have a word with the lads.

Coyne knew most of the Gardai at the local station. He had met them at one point or another in the course of his work, but he hated the humiliation of having to intercede on behalf of his own son. The worst thing was having to sit on the public bench. Coyne the temporary off-duty Garda, robbed of his status and told to sit and wait. The ignominy of it. Instead of ushering him straight into the main office, a Ban-Garda listened to him wearily at the hatch, ignored everything he said and told him to take a seat on the public bench.

Sergeant Corrigan eventually brought Coyne inside. They knew each other from a little spell they had spent together in Store Street Garda Station in the city centre. Corrigan was a tough policeman, always whistling with menacing intent. His nickname was Whistler, given to him by an unknown criminal and adopted by the rest of the force. It was Corrigan's style to leave long silences while questioning a suspect. Made people really uneasy to see a big Garda walking up and down the cell, whistling *The Homes of Donegal* to himself.

It's not an accident, Pat.

What?

Your son may have something to do with Tommy Nolan . . . The Sergeant stopped and rephrased what he wanted to say. He may be in a position to help us in our enquiries.

You must be joking, Coyne said. Let me talk to him.

Corrigan explained that there was a serious matter of some damage to property. Sabotage was the word he used at first before he changed it to vandalism. Malicious damage.

There was no mention of a stolen van. It did not even enter into the Garda log, because it was never reported missing. Some tiny nugget of wisdom shone through Jimmy's madness at the right moment, and he had parked the van on the seafront, where all the stolen cars usually ended up, sometimes burned out, sometimes crashed and looted, sometimes perfectly intact. Skipper Martin Davis did not have to go far to find it. The van was undamaged. But the holdall bag with the money was missing.

Jimmy Coyne never had to look for trouble. It came to him. He had been expelled from two good schools and barely scraped through his leaving cert exams. Now he was almost a year out of school with nothing to do but get drunk and wreck people's property. He was basically a good lad, Coyne always felt, just given to a temporary spell of self-destruction. Just like his father. But where Coyne had always been dedicated to sorting out the world, his son had a vocation for pure mayhem. The black hole of youth.

Hogan's yacht was the main focus of attention, for the moment. Councillor Hogan was suing for the damage and Jimmy Coyne was the obvious culprit. He had left his jacket in the cabin. A video store membership card inside belonging to Coyne.

I'd like to know where Hogan got the money for that yacht, Coyne muttered. As far as he was concerned, Councillor Hogan was a big fraud. He was the town killer, involved in every planning scandal going.

But this was the wrong thing to say. If anything, it made Coyne look like he had sent his son on a mission of destruction. Whistler stood like he was in a wax museum, warbling silently. Patience running out fast and his mouth shaped into a little O, ready for the last verse of *Avondale*, but the notes refusing to chime.

Jimmy sat in the cell with his head in his hands, more from a hangover than from remorse. Hardly even looked up when Coyne entered. So they sat in silence. There had never been very much communication between them.

Coyne had no words. He looked around the cell and saw for the first time what the world looked like from the reverse side. Even started reading some of the graffiti. Fuck the Law – Macker! Dope the Pope! Coyne and his son stared everywhere around that small cell but at each other. Until eventually Jimmy met his father's eyes by accident, in a brief glance. As though they had both been hiding behind bushes and suddenly had to give themselves up.

Coyne felt all the instincts of a father. Stupidity. Jealousy. Anger. Concern. His first thought was to ask his son about drugs.

Did you get yourself connected? he asked.

Jimmy was stunned by this new DJ vernacular. As though they could talk together openly in rhyming rap lyrics from now on. He thought he was elected.

Did you get yourself injected, is what I'm asking?

No! Jimmy responded.

Coyne maintained a stern face. What would Carmel say to all of this? What's more: what would her mother, Mrs Gogarty say? His reputation was on the line here.

You think you're cool, Coyne said.

Jimmy looked up. He saw that his father was a decent man. There was remorse and embarrassment in his eyes now.

I'm sorry, Dad!

So you should be, Coyne said. You know you've just fucked up any chance of me and your mother getting back together again.

Coyne was too soft-hearted. He could not be harsh with his son. He could not even bring himself to ask the big question. Did you have anything to do with Tommy Nolan's death?

Coyne sat listening to the familiar sounds of Garda activity outside – radio voices, computer terminals humming, people closing doors. He was close to tears, with his chin quivering. Not just because of this situation but the entire shock of what being in a police station meant to him now: a mixture of nostalgia and contempt for the profession which had taken up so much of his life. It made him more compassionate than ever before for his own son. He was desperately searching for more words to soften the impact of his anger towards him. Something more trivial. Warm. Something in rap language that would allow him to look into his son's eyes again and tell him that everything would be fine in the end. Something that rhymed with cool. It was the only way that Coyne had of keeping faith with his son in this difficult time.

You think you're cool, but you're only in the vestibule, Coyne said at last.

It was exactly the right thing to say – cross but hip. Jimmy sat up. It allowed them to look each other in the eye. Coyne got up and went across to his son. Put his arm around him.

You're only in the vestibule, son.

It was Carmel who ultimately got Jimmy out of trouble. She went straight down to the Chamber of Commerce and asked to speak to Councillor Hogan. Left her red Toyota parked outside the Town Hall. It was embarrassing having to go in to sit in front of him in his office. Hogan was looking at her legs.

She offered to pay for all the damage to the yacht, but he would not talk about money. He was more interested in her.

I hear you're into some kind of healing, he said, smiling.

Yes, Carmel said, totally surprised that her reputation had reached so far around the borough already.

I've got a very bad back, you know, Hogan appealed. Can't do anything with it at all.

How long have you had this?

Years! I've been all over the world. I even led a fact-finding delegation to Europe to study back pain. Nobody can do anything for me. It's an atrocity. There's no other word for it. An atrocity.

So they ended up talking about lower back pain and osteoporosis. It was Carmel who ended up offering sympathy and solace to Councillor Hogan. She was off, asking intimate questions about his diet, exercise, medical history. She soon had him bending over and arching back for her. All kinds of people turned instantly humble in front of a healer.

What kind of healing do you do? he asked.

Stones, she said. I do things with stones.

There was no need to mention the grubby business of the yacht any more. Carmel said she would insist on paying for the damage, but Councillor Hogan waved his hand. The charges were dropped, without question. All it took was a phone call. It was sub-verbal.

The next thing on Carmel's mind was to straighten Jimmy out. There was little she could do for her estranged husband, but she could set her own son on the right road at least. So when Jimmy was released she brought him directly down to the Haven nursing home and got him a job. Told him to stay at home for a while so she could keep an eye on him. She was not going to spend the whole summer looking after a delinquent son. One delinquent ex-husband was enough for the time being. There was no need to get angry or triumphant about any of this. She was being practical, that's all.

On top of everything else, Coyne was a bit of an insomniac. Middle of the night, he sat bolt upright in the bed, talking to himself like a deranged man. He was in no mood to make any more terrorist phone calls and shuffled around the flat instead, muttering and staring out the window at the ivy-covered garden walls at the back of the houses.

He was wide awake, confronted by a particular image of the famine which he had heard of in school and which still haunted him – how a dead couple were found inside a cottage with the woman's head cradled in the man's lap for the last bit of warmth. The final act of unselfish loyalty against such a cruel fate. Coyne could not get past that point in history.

He searched the whole kitchen but found nothing. Not even a cracker. What kind of housekeeping was this when he woke up at night like a famished man?

He rang Carmel, got her up out of bed and started babbling to her over the phone. 3:33 – the time of revelation.

For Godsake, Pat! This is crazy.

I'm starving, he said.

Jesus, Pat. Are you still in therapy?

Carmel was rubbing her eyes, speaking in woolly voice on the other end of the line, trying to sound more angry than she really was. This was a serious invasion of privacy.

Pat, what are you trying to say? What are you calling me for like a baby in the middle of the night?

I need you, Carmel. I can't live without you.

Go back to sleep, Pat. Jesus! Is that psychologist any use?

Carmel tried to calm him down. Was this another annual suicide alert, she wondered. She talked to him for a while until he began to sound normal again. Brought him back down to earth.

I forgot to do the shopping, he said.

I don't believe it, Pat, she laughed. You mean to tell me you phoned me up looking for food.

Please Carmel. I haven't eaten anything all day.

What do you expect? Meals on wheels?

It's an emergency, Carmel. There's nothing.

Is this some trick, Pat? If you're just trying to get me over to your flat, you can forget it. Because that would be really vile, and I'd never forgive you.

I swear, Carmel.

Going into Coyne's flat would have been a step beyond. Forbidden grounds. Mrs Gogarty, who was working against Coyne like a renegade in his own former home, kept telling Carmel it would be a big mistake ever to enter Coyne's lair. Put your foot inside that door and you'll never come out again.

Carmel was still half asleep as she drove the car.

Coyne stood at the door and looked at his ex-wife with a kind of haunted expression in his eyes. Her hair was in a mess. The dressing gown showed under the green coat, and she wore shoes with no socks. She was annoyed that he had forced her to get out and walk up the steps, having to ring the bell and hand over the sandwich at the door instead of him coming out to the car.

You can give me back the lunchbox when you're finished, she said.

She took the opportunity in return to examine her ex-husband, fully dressed, but looking a little harassed and thin. He was obviously not eating properly. Going into decline since the separation. She was hoping he would go for acupuncture, get himself sorted out and stop being a burden on her conscience.

Coyne asked her if she wanted to come inside.

She asked about his health. A neutral enquiry.

I'm not sick, he exclaimed suspiciously.

What are you off work for, Pat? For Godsake, just listen to your chest.

Coyne smiled. He held up the sandwich box and winked at her. Thanks!

You don't take care of yourself, she said. I'm not going to allow you to take that attitude towards your health. Your energy has become trapped.

Ah now, Carmel. Take it easy.

Coyne didn't like the sound of this consultation on the doorstep. He knew where it was leading to. How *are* you? How do you *feel*? Soon she would start going on about psycho-neuro-immunology again – all the stuff about prolonged stress in the aftermath of trauma. She seemed to be overheating a little these days, using strange new words that whooped like a car alarm around Coyne's head. Words like energy flow and centering. She said Coyne would have to embark on a journey within, whatever the hell that meant. He had lost the map.

You know me, Carmel. Anything that can't be cured by a pint is not worth curing.

That's where you're wrong, Pat. You've got to cross the threshold.

What threshold?

Coyne deeply mistrusted this new faith-healing vernacular. These were the words of betrayal. Besides, there was too much healing going on in this town. People being healed who had nothing wrong with them in the first place, except that they might have required a good kick in the arse. Too many strange and unnatural practices going on. One thing was certain: Coyne was going on no journey within; or without, for that matter. And he was not going across any shaggin' threshold either.

We're messing, he said, looking into her eyes.

Carmel backed away from this sudden rush of intimacy. Protecting herself at all costs, she turned and walked back towards the car.

Carmel, it's you and me, he said with great feeling, following her out through the gate.

Is this what you got me up in the middle of the night for? She turned back and faced him on the pavement. You're not hungry at all. You just tricked me into coming over.

She was determined not to slide back into this marriage. Losing all her independence. Having to live with Coyne's madness again. Listening to him shouting at the radio every day. Indulging his theories, nursing his phobias, and watching him cast his overwhelming spell of paranoia and doom all over the house. She had to keep things on a practical level.

Coyne stood on the pavement with the lunchbox in his hand, bending down to try and talk to her through the window. But Carmel started the car and drove off. He wanted to tell her that her dressing gown was hanging out through the door of the car. Flapping as she went around the corner out of sight.

Carmel's mother felt Coyne was simply beyond help. She prayed for him. He was beyond redemption. She behaved as though her son-in-law was dead already.

Each night as she knelt down alone at her bed and began the prayers for the deceased, like a rap hit litany of departed souls. Coyne the living dead man, walking around like one of the lost souls in purgatory.

Dear Lord have mercy on the souls of my dear Paddy, Nance, Eva, Mammy, Daddy, Granny, Auntie Mary, Auntie Essie, Eamon, Ned, Uncle Charlie, Uncle Paddy, Auntie Olive, Uncle Dan, Uncle Tom, Uncle Denis, Uncle Mick, Auntie Girlie, Auntie Olive, Father Moynihan, Frank Donnelly, Kathleen Boyce, Lilly Whitelaw, Jenny Pollock . . . for Aidan Martin, Father Joyce, Father Brady, Father Collins, Bobby Hayes, Mary Fuller, Michael Collins, Sean South, for poor Kevin Barry and for Pat Coyne and all the souls in purgatory especially Lord for those who have no one to pray for them in the hour of their death. Amen.

Coyne's therapist, Ms Clare Dunford had her own professional anxieties about his frame of mind. She had never met so much resistance before in her entire career and had to devote a lot of attention to his case; putting on the rubber gloves, in other words. She wore glasses on a chain and looked over the rims at Coyne as if to say – Listen here, my friend. I've dealt with all kinds of maniacs in here, alcoholics, wife-beaters, rapists, murderers, you name it. I'm not going to be put off that easily by you, Mr Coyne. I'll sort you out if it kills me.

She was not convinced that the trauma of the fire alone, or even the break-up with Carmel, could have caused so much damage in itself. There had to be some other problem underneath that would stop Coyne from going back to work and behaving like a normal individual. Something substantial that went back to Coyne's childhood, perhaps. The fire was merely a trigger.

She tried to explain to Coyne that he had most probably become separated from himself. Her idea was that after the fire and the failure associated with this event, Coyne had walked out on himself and slammed the door. His inner self was really angry and vowed never to go back again. Basically, there were two Coynes now: the flesh and blood Coyne who went for a pint and lived in the real world and occasionally thought about committing suicide; and the other Coyne who had started messing about and being terribly difficult and looking down with great condescension on the real Coyne. They were like feuding brothers with separate entrances to the same house: the outside Coyne refusing to speak to the poor flesh and blood Coyne, because he had let him down on the day of the fire, through no fault of his own.

Coyne was an awkward subject. He was against all this psychoanalysis and feared categories. Next thing they'd be saying he was still in love with his mother, or that he was schizophrenic, or autistic or something. He hated the notion that there might be a recognizable syndrome or description for his state of mind. The only reason he was attending these sessions was to make himself eligible for compensation. Coyne's solicitor had advised him just to go along with the treatment, even if it was doing him no good.

The state was going to pay out some serious money in aggravated damages.

Ms Dunford was in her late forties with a round, ill-defined shape. She usually wore a loose, silk blouse and blue-grey tweed skirt. Her bottom row of teeth jutted out a little further than the top row, and Coyne couldn't get over the idea that her face was upside down. Every now and again he wanted to bend over and see if she looked any better from underneath. As well as that, she wore massive shoes, and Coyne imagined large, webbed feet inside them, like a giant duck.

You're not fooling me, Ms Duckfoot.

He wasn't taken in by her motherly approach either. Coyne was thinking compensation as he answered all her routine questions with the maximum degree of neurosis, presenting an alarming impression of total human wreck. Depression. Irrational fears. Memory loss. Lack of concentration. Post-traumatic stress disorder! By Jesus, Coyne had them all.

Tell me about the fire, she said.

I'm trying to forget about it, he said.

You were on duty, weren't you? You attempted a rescue.

If you don't mind, Coyne said. I don't want to re-enact the whole thing again.

You've got to let go, she said. You're driving with the handbrake on, Pat.

Coyne looked up at her with a stunned expression on his face. Where did she learn all this cartoon psychology, he wanted to know. All these pert little phrases. All this shaggin' common sense. There was nothing worse than amateurs spouting superstition, pretending it was science. She tried to placate him by putting the proceedings on first name terms. He could call her Clare from now on. She sat up on her desk. Perched on the ledge with giant feet dangling.

You know, there's an old Chinese saying that you can't see your own chin, she said.

Here we go again!

Coyne was astonished by this latest remark. What in the name of Jesus was she getting at? What had Coyne's chin got to do with anything. All I can see is your chin, Ms Duckfoot, and it looks like a giant strawberry.

You can never grasp everything, she explained. It's a mistake to try and examine your own soul too carefully.

Listen here, you Jungian monster. I don't want to be normal. I don't want to be cured. I don't want to go back to work. All I want is the compensation. And so what if I can't see my own chin. I can't see my own arse either, but that doesn't stop me from grasping it, now does it?

Tommy Nolan's funeral was a quiet event. Coyne and a number of people loitering around the crematorium to hear the priest say a few charismatic words about the soul of Tommy Nolan. A great character who would be limping no more in heaven. A man who would be missed by the whole community. Some people in attendance who hardly even said hello to Tommy while he was alive. McCurtain from the Port and Docks board was there, pretending he had been a lifelong friend.

And more surprising again was the fact that the burial at sea had been organized by trawlerman, Martin Davis.

On a windy, early summer afternoon, around a dozen people stood on the deck of the *Lolita*. The priest remarked that it was strictly against the law to cast the ashes out like this. But he was defying it for Tommy's sake. The breakdown between church and state.

So that's how the ashes were disbursed in Dublin Bay. With the Superferry passing by a few hundred yards away, and the Dublin mountains in the distance behind the city. A decade of the rosary carrying out across the water. Another homily about the tragic nature of his untimely death and

Tommy's sister casting the white dust and shards of bleached bone out from the stern of the boat with tears in her eyes. Seagulls coming to investigate. Hovering over a choppy grave.

The real farewell for Tommy Nolan took place later on that night at the Anchor Bar. Pints all round for the lads. The place had never been so jammed before, because people were of the firm belief that the only real way to honour the passing of Tommy was to get legless and locked out of their skulls. Mouldy in memory of the dead. That's what Tommy would have done himself.

Coyne was mute as a stone and full of resentment. He knew that Tommy's death was no accident, and anyone who took part in this event was under suspicion. There was something strange about the fact that the skipper of the *Lolita* was buying pints for everyone. Magnanimous Martin Davis was hiding something, standing centre stage at the Anchor Bar with his arm around Marlene Nolan.

This thing wasn't over and finished yet, as far as Coyne was concerned.

The rumour went around that Tommy had come across some foreign youths at the harbour. A conspiracy theory began to develop that he had been dumped in the harbour by a stag party on the return to the Superferry. A random attack on a poor defenceless man, killed for no reason. Tommy Nolan knew the harbour too well to have fallen in of his own accord. People liked a conspiracy theory.

Everybody was langered. Sooner or later, McCurtain made his way over to Coyne and started talking indiscriminately into his ear, expanding on his own past glories. There was one of them in every bar, and Kelly's Anchor Bar was no exception. Given half a chance, McCurtain soon got down to boasting about his life as a playboy. Telling Coyne how

32

the women of the borough used to go mad for him. Making himself out to be some kind of legendary Irish Don Juan.

There were more husbands after me than Indians were after General Custer, he announced with a smell of diesel on his breath.

Sure, Coyne muttered.

Why this sudden rush of nationwide honesty, he thought. I mean, why couldn't people keep things to themselves any more? On the radio; on TV: everybody exposing themselves and trying to come to terms with their own psychological junk. Go and expose yourself to the Blessed Sacrament. Why don't you?

The women used to place bets on me, you know, McCurtain bragged.

Do me a favour, Coyne said, because he'd heard all these fantasies before, many times. Go home and decompose. Go on, back to your crypt, McCurtain.

But the thick-skinned Irish Casanova would not go away and Coyne was drawn into the unavoidable confrontation. One of those drunken funeral debates that took place at the bar with everyone listening in. Some vital point that had to be hammered out, as though Coyne had a civic duty to challenge McCurtain with the facts. Let him know that Coyne stood on the side of aggrieved husbands.

You're like the Irish Elk, Coyne said.

What are you on about now? McCurtain said, half walking away.

You're going into extinction, Coyne explained by way of a parable. Will I tell you what happened to the Irish Elk?

McCurtain pricked up his ears. He was ready for this kind of schoolboy abuse.

Go on, hit me!

You want to know why he became extinct? Coyne went on. Sex, that's why. Too much sex on his mind.

The barman was listening in, smiling to himself. This was a good one. He even alerted the staff from the lounge next

33

door to come in and catch this. Coyne talking extinction. Calling McCurtain an Irish Elk. Coyne was dead serious. Never before had the subject of sex been so openly debated in the Irish pub. Coyne delivering a vital message to General fucking Custer with masterful brevity and eloquence. Famous last words, spoken on the night of the funeral, in the shadow of mortality.

The Irish Elk never stopped thinking about sex, Coyne announced. He was obsessed with nothing else. That's what killed him.

Would you listen to him, McCurtain smirked.

The barman stood holding up a glass in his hand. Stalled with incomprehension.

I'm not joking you, Coyne said, raising his voice. It was one big snuff movie for the Irish Elk. Because he was so interested in attracting the female and fighting off other males, that his antlers kept getting bigger. That was his downfall. Couldn't run around any more. Every time he bent down to drink water, he couldn't get his head up again. I'm telling you, they found a whole load of ancient elk horns by a lake up there in Wicklow.

Stick to bottled water, the barman said at last.

Would you fuck off, McCurtain bawled. Coyne, you're like an anthropologist. What's wrong with you?

You're in a cul-de-sac, Coyne said.

McCurtain winked at the barman. Exchanged a grin of consensus. Then McCurtain started laughing his head off, cackling like he needed to have his head examined.

Coyne had delivered his message with crisp profundity. That would give the bastard something to think about, he said to himself. The barmen too. Each man before the jury of his own sex life. Every one of them reflecting on the decline of the Irish Elk at the height of his powers. Living on an island, with hardly any predators. His own worst enemy. Running like the prince of the species across bogs and mountains. Barking through the darkness of the oak

34

forest. Standing with his heavy antlers up and his sad eyes staring out through the silent intimacy of dawn.

Somebody had brought a guitar. There was no band playing next door that night, so it was decided to do Tommy Nolan the honour of a few songs. They sang *Galveston*, because Tommy had always been a bit of a cowboy at heart, a freak character from some memorable Western, a humble man, making a living in the shadow of the great legends – the local sheriffs, baddies, barmen, molls and dollar men. Perhaps he had been abducted by the Indians as a child and left to stalk the borough like an enigmatic figure with a strange past that nobody wanted to know. Until he was dead, at least. For a moment the Anchor Bar became a saloon as they sang Tommy's favourite number. *Three wheels on my wagon – and I'm still rolling along* . . .

Later it was *So Long, Marianne*, which they sang like some fiery republican ballad. And *Massachusetts*. In deep male voices. Belting it out with such masculine pride and testosterone dignity that you'd think it had to do with some ambush in the war of independence, a shoot-out with the Black and Tans.

I'm going back to Maaah-ssechusetts . . .

In the name of Jaysus, Coyne thought. You can't do that with a hippie song. It's meant to be all about peace and love and banality, with eunuch harmonies. You can't start that macho growl at somebody's funeral either. Strumming the guitar like an anti-aircraft gun. Pack of granite gobshites, turning a flower power hit into a Provo marching song.

And then it was McCurtain's turn to sing. The great Irish Casanova with the rebel heart who never discharged a shot in his life. The overspecialized Irish Elk, facing extinction and singing *The Fields of Athenry* with huge passion and fervour. McCurtain and his pals were in an evolutionary cul-de-sac, crooning the anthem of republican, auto-erotic perfection. A mythological country between the sheets. The great, all-time fantasy ride.

High-low, the fields of Athenry . . . They clapped and cheered in frenzied admiration as McCurtain raised his arms in the air, the bastard. Out of breath with post-coital exertion.

But then, at last came something European. A Russian fisherman offered to do a solo number. There was a visiting trawler in the bay that night, a big factory ship which had brought Russians all over the town, reciprocating with more free pints. Must have thought there was a funeral in Ireland every night. Just like at home.

Hang on, lads! Pushkin here wants to take the floor.

A man with dark brown rims around his eyes and hollow cheekbones started singing *Danny Boy*. Chest inflating. Letting out a gale of breath like it was going to bring ye back all the way to his own home town of Noril'sk.

Oh, Dannyol Boy. . . From glyen to glyen . . .

The crowd in the Anchor Bar was stunned. McCurtain said it was a travesty.

Bleedin' mockery, he growled. The Russian couldn't sing and shouldn't be let. If they hadn't put up all the free pints, they'd be turfed out of the pub. Back to the factory ship with a filleting knife in the back.

Fair play to you, Coyne encouraged the singer. Anything to defy the bellowing elk.

McCurtain muttered on about the Russians as new invaders, fishing every benthic inch and fathom around Erin's green shores, cleaning out the entire fish stocks. They had some audacity to come into the Anchor Bar and crucify *Danny Boy* like it was a karaoke night.

But everybody else loved this new rendition. It was the greatest version of *Danny Boy* they had ever heard. An old song of emigration, rescued from the graveyard of trite emotion and brought back to life with the fresh lungs of Russian loneliness. Great big Russian vowels hanging in the

36

smoky blue air and the whole pub bulging with the sound of this man's epic voice. Veins standing out on his Caucasian forehead. And people joining in, even from the lounge next door. *Danny Boy* – from Donegal to the Urals.

Come forward! I want to come forward.

A number of witnesses had 'come forward' to say they had seen something going on the night Tommy Nolan was killed. A woman from one of the new apartment blocks overlooking the harbour said she had witnessed a struggle on the quay. From her bedroom window, no less than eight hundred yards away, she had seen two people either fighting or embracing. Later she saw people running. This was corroborated by a motorist who reported seeing car headlights on the pier and some youths fighting. Both gave a similar time frame – around 2:30 a.m.

Sergeant Corrigan was in his element, like the whistling gypsy rover, doing house to house enquiries all around the flash apartments. He was chatting up the harbour police, nightwatchmen, caretakers, cooks; anyone remotely involved in harbour activity. Men in yellow coats. Torch carriers. Reflective sash and luminous donkey jacket wearers. He was seen drifting around the boat yards and yacht clubs, making a nuisance of himself all day. Then back to the woman in the apartment, just to confirm whether she had said 'struggle' or 'scuffle' in her statement. His handwriting was as bad as his whistling.

Tommy Nolan's post-mortem had revealed very little. Officially, it was not quite a murder enquiry yet, but Corrigan was uneasy about the whole thing. The picture was not plumb, let's say. The funeral and a rousing farewell at the Anchor Bar were not sufficient to put Tommy Nolan's soul to rest, because society demanded some narrative conclusion. The full stop. Tommy Nolan had left behind a bit of a semi-colon, and Sergeant Corrigan was out there trying to finish the sentence with the right punctuation. He was besieged by the flat syntax of cop buzzwords and phrases, such as trying to close the book. Piece of the jigsaw missing. At the end of the day. In the heel of the hunt. He was always using words like complexion – Oh that puts a different complexion on the matter. He was living in the world of the school textbook where Sean and Nora were always playing with the ball, Mammy was smiling in the kitchen making sandwiches while Daddy was outside mowing the lawn, and Rolo, the dog, was yelping at a cat in the tree. Something was not right in the early reader.

The problem was that all of this was pointing straight at Jimmy Coyne. According to Corrigan's linear logic, he was up to his neck in it. Corrigan was up at Coyne's flat on Cross-eyed Park, whistling silently in the living room. Prompting. Trying to make Coyne talk about his son. Double-checking statements and generally wasting everybody's time. You think we have nothing better to do than listen to you whistling some really thick, country-evangelical tune like *What if God was one of us?*

What has God got to do with us, you gobshite? That was Coyne's chorus. If God was one of us, he'd be a thick Garda sergeant, no question of it. A red-faced know-all, whistling through a bullet hole in his face.

I'm just trying to clarify a few matters, Corrigan explained.

Then he began to work up a line-of-enquiry. Just to demonstrate his capacity for lateral thinking, he looked around the front room for clues, took in the picture of Coyne in uniform on the mantelpiece and behaved as though he was still treating Coyne like he was one of the lads, only to turn on him with a tricky little question. Like a left hook. Real Garda tripwire tactics. Straight out of the manual.

I believe you went to school with him? Corrigan asked.

Yeah, Coyne answered. So?

38

Coyne had nothing to hide, but he was far too bellicose. Definitely uncool. He should have waited a moment and then given a more composed reply. He just didn't want to fit in with the logic of daily Irish grammar any more. Those formative links that went all the way back to school. He didn't subscribe to neat Garda solutions. Motivation. Causality.

Sergeant Corrigan turned his back and looked out the window. In the hope that Coyne could not see what he was doing, he started picking his nose. Coyne couldn't believe it. This was not some discreet little knuckle wipe or nosewing scratch. This was explicit soil excavation. Hardcore. Over eighteens. Corrigan's index finger penetrating diligently and his head tilted conveniently to the left in order to dislodge big stalactites on to the floor.

Should have seen the look on Coyne's face. You'd think he'd just been handed the joke shop lighter, with the electric current running halfway up his arm. Pulled his fist back suddenly as though he was going to box the sergeant in the back of the head. Give it up! Stop that unnatural practice in my home. Go and carry out your dig in somebody else's place, you disgusting bastard.

Corrigan turned and looked Coyne in the eye. Held up the foraging finger and pointed towards the door. Coyne was more interested in the finger than anything else. Followed it wherever Corrigan pointed.

I think your son is involved in this, Pat. There may be a connection.

Forget it, Coyne exploded.

Calm down. I'm only telling you what I think.

Corrigan got ready to leave. He put his hand on the doorknob.

I'm only trying to warn you, he said. As a member of the force and all that. You should have a word with him. He knows something, Corrigan said.

Jimmy Coyne settled down very quickly at the Haven. He was transformed. He was suddenly making money and found the two things that gave meaning to his life – love and morphine.

From the first day, he took to gerontology with great dedication. The exclusivity of being the sole youth among old people gave him a sense of immortality. They were on the way out – he was on the way up. He appreciated the feeling of indestructible health bestowed on him by the aged. Even the simple pleasure of passing by an old man on the lino corridor made Jimmy feel like he was travelling at ninety miles an hour, accelerating into the future.

His duties consisted mostly of helping sisters and nurses to lift the infirm in and out of beds and baths. Driving wheelchairs around. Bringing patients to Mass and back, up and down in the lift.

Jimmy enjoyed a sense of vigour and power, not just of his sudden athleticism, but also of moral superiority. At the Haven nursing home, he quickly assumed the role of God. Around these old people, he became the Lord of the Haven – a figure of immortality, bursting with the insurrection of youth. He was in a position to grant favours and to punish. If he felt that one of the old people was becoming too demanding, he would send them back to the end of the queue. As he passed by the rooms in his white coat and heard the helpless calls from inside, begging him to pick up a book or a ball of wool, he exercised divine power to leave them in their misery, or to reach into their fusty, apple-smelling rooms and help.

It was like final judgement day, with Jimmy Coyne as the Almighty. At times he was extremely kind and warm-hearted. But these old people occasionally incurred his wrath, and he would be forced to exact revenge. He punished old Dr Spain for being so cruel to his bedridden wife who was unable to defend herself. He left him turned the wrong way round in the church, with the brakes on his wheelchair, leaving him looking away from the altar with a smouldering pipe in his jacket pocket.

Little incidents like that made Jimmy's life worth while.

There was also access to pharmaceuticals. And Nurse Boland. She was a lot older than he was, a refugee from a marriage in Cork who had settled in Dublin. He spent every day of the week changing bed sheets with her. He liked her accent. He discovered that he liked to be on the left-hand side, because there was a small gap in her buttoned-up uniform that allowed him to see inside. You couldn't keep Jimmy out of the Haven nursing home.

In due course, Jimmy paid his debt to society. With his first wage packet he was determined to pay off the damage to Councillor Hogan's yacht, more for his mother's sake than his own. The job at the nursing home seemed to have changed his outlook on life and he became generous and thoughtful. His first wage packet knew no bounds and he bought gifts all round, for his mother and his grandmother. A new kettle for the flat.

Even then, there was still enough money left for Jimmy to buy new clothes for himself. His spell of nihilism was replaced by a spell of opulence. A golden age of affluence. He had become cool at last, buying the right clothes, drinking the right drinks.

It was really all about being cool, Coyne thought. Cool probably meant the same as being 'holy' used to mean. Being right and sacred and with God and all that stuff. Nowadays it was all to do with listening to the right music and being with the right women. 'Cool' was the new word for 'holy'. And Jimmy looked like he had just come out of confession, with a halo over his head. Or some kind of exclamation mark emanating from his scalp. In a state of grace! Walking with a new swagger of divine self-confidence, 'I've got the power' emblazoned on his face.

Jimmy was so full of generosity and good will that he

became a bit of a philanthropist and extended his largesse to the marginalized sections of the community too. He stopped outside the shopping centre and gave the poet with the four dogs and the dreadlocks some money. People in the borough usually had more sympathy for the poet's dogs. But Jimmy gave him a bunch of dollars.

In God we trust, the poet said in amazement.

Don't mention it, Jimmy said.

The poet jumped up and started reciting bits of Yeats, bits of Heaney, and bits of his own garbled up work with renewed self-esteem and enthusiasm through his stained teeth. A listener with money. This was too good to be true. The cognoscenti had discovered him at last and he recited his work in a low monotone voice, almost inaudible at times with the weight of passion and pathos until he was whispering into Jimmy Coyne's ear. He tried to force his portfolio of scribbled gems on him, but Jimmy wanted nothing in return for his feckless donation. He smiled and walked off again, on his way back towards the Haven nursing home, looking over his shoulder as he went.

The banks were shut and the poet with four docile dogs and dreadlocks had difficulty in finding a shop to accept the dollars. They all thought it was fake money. Even the man in the local off-licence was reluctant. Held the notes up in the air with no idea what the exchange rate was. McDonald's politely told the poet to fuck off. They didn't want him feeding Big Macs to his dogs outside the door either, because the customers might start thinking about what they were eating.

So that's how the dreadlock poet ended up in the Anchor Bar, late the same evening, desperately trying to persuade the barmen to look up the paper and strike a rate.

We're not a bank, the barman was saying.

Did you rob a tourist? one of the men asked. But the docile poet was in no humour for jokes and the Anchor Bar finally obliged him with a pint. Plain ham sandwiches for the dogs tied up to the drainpipe in the laneway alongside the pub.

The news travelled fast. Somebody at the Anchor Bar was aware of the significance of dollars entering the local economy. Word got around to skipper Martin Davis and he came up to have a look for himself. Ordered a pint and casually asked the barman if he could have a look at the money.

Bud in a fuckin' sheasamh, he said to himself. It was genuine American money all right. And the docile poet was sitting in the snug, babbling to himself again with a pint and a short in front of him.

Mongi O Doherty made it out from the city to the Anchor Bar before closing time.

Hold him there, he said on his mobile in an up-beat tone. He had a feeling it wouldn't be too long before the money forced its way back into circulation. Money had gravitational pull. Money had homing instincts.

I want to hear some of that poetry, he said. Nobel stuff. With lots of Greek gods and Greek mythology. All that shite about Persephone and Philoctetes.

Mongi didn't actually make an appearance at the Anchor Bar himself. He waited outside patiently until the poet came out in his own good time. You couldn't rush these artists. Skipper Martin Davis stayed well out of sight; he was a local man with a familiar face.

When the poet stumbled out at last, he was gently led down the lane in an exalted state of perception. He had hit a phase of great clarity and prolific creativity. He waved to the four docile muses tied to the drainpipe and was already climbing into an empty skip before he knew what was happening. For a moment, he thought he was stepping into a Greek ship. There was nothing inside except for a few bits of broken wood and cast-iron guttering. It was very private, and perfect for a spontaneous poetry reading. Mongi climbed in with him to be his audience. His hollow laugh echoing around the galleon as he walked up and down, while the poet sat on the floor of the skip, leaning back in fear and handing over a fistful of dollars from his pocket. The dogs were whimpering in the background.

I thought you guys were suppose to live in penury, Mongi bawled as he searched through the grubby portfolio. Where did you get this money?

There was a sudden loss of imagination. The poet could not think of an answer. Said he thought it was a tourist who gave it to him. A fan maybe?

How could you have a fan?

Take the money, the poet blubbered. It interferes with my art anyway. Keep the portfolio too. Some powerful stuff in there. Really good ones that would scald your hand while you were reading them.

Never get a proper bleedin' answer, Mongi muttered.

He was losing his cool. He was an entrepreneur, with no time for all this subtlety and reflection. He counted the money and put it in his pocket. Where was the rest of it? he wanted to know. Found a piece of wood with a bent six-inch nail sticking out of it. Dropped it in favour of a piece of cast-iron guttering which looked more inspirational. He knocked the poet over and put his pump-up runner across his face. Started belting scrap metal into his shins and kneecaps until the lyrics came spouting out through his trousers in blood red ink. We're supporting enough of you bastards. You do nothing for this country. You're in every pub, dead or alive, staring at people while they drink their pints. You're all a waste of food and drink, he shouted, while the docile poet was howling haikus. Stream of unconscious.

Coyne felt guilty about his son. Since Jimmy had been involved with the law, he thought of all the things he should have done with him while he was still a boy. All the fishing trips they never went on. All the football matches that other dads had brought their sons to but Coyne had no time for. He thought of all the casual conversations he should have had with Jimmy. All the moments when they might have laughed together.

It was too late now.

Or perhaps not. Perhaps Coyne could make another last-minute effort to bond with his son by taking him up to the Dublin mountains. One Saturday morning, he got him up at the crack of dawn to make egg sandwiches. Dozens of them. Enough for a whole Scout camp. They got to the outskirts of the city by bus and started walking along forest paths, not saying much. Just acknowledging each other's presence. With the wind whistling in their ears.

Maybe it was really a way of getting back in touch with Carmel. All day he walked with his son in silence. They were completely lost up there in the mountains, in awe of the emptiness. All that rocky and barren space with muted colours. The most deserted landscape on earth. Not far enough away from the suburbs to be exotic and not close enough to feel like home. It was nowhere. A bleak, disused back garden on the edge of the city.

Coyne was desperately trying to be close to his son but missing it by a mile.

Look at the stones and the rocks, he said, pointing to a moss-covered boulder with age spots of lichen marks, like an old man's face. The landscape was full of rocks. There was nothing to appreciate only rocks and stones, and Coyne spoke about them with great passion, as though he had never seen them before.

All these years in the Gardai, Coyne said, putting his hand on Jimmy's shoulder, I've been blind. I never understood the significance of ordinary things like rocks.

The breeze across the open spaces was relentless as they sat down to eat the egg sandwiches. It hummed as Coyne unwrapped tinfoil packages and blew a hollow note from the rim of Jimmy's Coke bottle as he placed it on the ground between his feet. They smiled at each other briefly, and then looked away again, out over the purple distance of the bald moutains. In that moment they were closer than they had ever been before, united by the ritual of food.

Except that Coyne could not go for too long without having to talk. He feared the silence. Felt the need to make some kind of speech about the petrified beauty of the place. These rocks were timeless. Rocks were all that mattered. Rocks were kings. They outclassed all the false building materials of the city, and Coyne talked about the purity of rocks with such emotional ballast that it made Jimmy cringe and long to be back in the Haven nursing home. Jimmy was begging the aliens to land right there in that desolate spot and take him away, rescue him from his father's sobbing intimacy.

Think of the infinity contained in those rocks, Coyne said with caramel sentimentality. The history they've witnessed. The link with the past.

Jimmy started wrapping up the left-over sandwiches. Anything to release him from this choking passion.

I know, I talk too much, Coyne said.

And then, at the last minute, he suddenly remembered his fatherly duty. Carmel had urged him to have a man-to-man talk with Jimmy. On top of all he had said about rocks, he tried to introduce Jimmy to the facts of life. At the worst possible moment, in a casual, laddish way, Coyne started asking him what a condom was. Then started talking about real love with tears in his eyes.

It's a hoor to be in love, he said.

I wouldn't know, Jimmy answered.

You'll find out one of these days, son. It's a hoor to be in love.

As they descended from the barren heights into the more

populated foothills, the forest sanctity of their walk began to disappear. Something about the sight of civilization put an end to the special status they had achieved on their journey together. The escape was foiled. Jimmy saw that his father hated going back home. Expected him to go straight into a monologue about low-density, car-dependent housing schemes that had ruined the outskirts of the city. But instead, they had something else to think about.

Who should they run into but Sergeant Corrigan? On his day off. After trekking all over the mountain range, they came back down to greener spring meadows where people stepped out of their cars for a breath of fresh air.

They felt entitled to a kind of sad elitism as they re-entered society. They had endured the intimacy of rock and bogland. They had endured each other. They had survived silence and discovered a deep spiritual link with the emptiness and the wind and the sun sloping across open spaces. A brown landscape disappearing into the postcard distance over ridges. And beyond, banks of clouds that looked like even taller mountains rising up into the sky. All that melancholy attachment was carried back into the city by Coyne like a flame of resentment. What they had to contend with now was not anonymity and loneliness, but recognition. They were welcomed back into the arms of banality by Brendan Corrigan and his family.

Corrigan out there playing the father with his own two sons, aged around eleven and twelve. He was virtually sending a message to Coyne, saying – look, I'm a father too. And I've got every right to walk around here as well, you know. You're not the only one.

It destroyed the experience of being alone in the mountains. The bastard had conspired to be there when Coyne came back. Just when Coyne had created a fragile bond with his son, they were dragged brutally back into the crass reality of everyday existence.

Coyne – the man without subtext.

And what was that in Sergeant Corrigan's hand? A hurling stick. Coyne could not believe his eyes as he watched Corrigan walking up the grassy slope, taking out his *sliotar*, giving it an almighty whack and sending the ball up into the meadow for the boys to chase after. Two strong young sons, running as fast as they could to get there first. Searching around eagerly in the grass until one of them found it and they came running back again. Off-duty Sergeant Corrigan with a fierce red face on him as he repeated the whole thing all over again. Whack. Sending the ball in a beautiful arc all the way up along the slope again with the boys chasing and yelping.

I mean, what the fuck was this in aid of? Coyne thought. The man didn't even see the symbolism of what he was doing. Training the sons of Ireland to fetch, like dogs. Like greyhounds.

From his hospital bed, the docile poet renounced all forms of personal wealth. He made a vow of poverty. Never again would he allow money, and especially foreign money, to corrupt his creative soul. From now on, he told the nurses trying to wash his dreadlocks, he would rely only on the hospitality of the people. He would return to the ancient bardic order of praising those who lavished courtesy on him and heaping derision on those who abused him. He was writing sonnets to the nurses, even if they wouldn't let him smoke. And God help the man who worked him over in the skip, because the poet was far from docile with words and was already working on a red hot, scrotum-burning, invective epic against Mongi O Doherty. Though he didn't know the name of his tormentor, the poet wished him the most eloquent forms of ill health and everlasting death throes – may you live for ever on a life-support machine, may you watch yourself dying in the mirror.

The poet was reluctant to show the curse-poem to anyone before it was finished. Detectives were mystified because he gave no explanation apart from the fact that there seemed to be a bad omen around American currency. In God we trust, at our own peril. In God we trust to snatch the money right out of our hands again. In God we trust, the tight-fisted bastard!

I cursed all foreign money . . . the poet began to sing, and Sergeant Corrigan finally made a vague connection with the exchange of dollars at the Anchor Bar, but there the trail foundered in a fog of superstition and lyrical obfuscation.

I can't ascertain a thing from that poet, Corrigan said.

Coyne went to visit Tommy Nolan's sister Marlene, a small nervous woman with a ponytail and freckles all over her face. She wore a shiny tracksuit with FORCE written across the front. Spoke with a smoked-out voice and lit up various cigarettes that she never finished as she brought Coyne inside and talked to him about Tommy.

There was a huge TV in the living room.

He loved watching snooker, Marlene explained.

There were pictures on the mantelpiece of Marlene and Tommy as children. Happy times by the harbour with their father. Another one with all their cousins outside, on the street. Now she was the sister of a murdered man.

The Gardai had already gone through everything in Tommy's room. Coyne was proud of him for keeping his place so tidy. He admired Tommy's sense of order. His snooker cue standing in the corner. A shelf with Western videos. And one of the neatest toolboxes ever. A masterpiece of originality and adaptation: a six-pack wine carton with a handle that had been remodelled as a toolbox containing a hammer, screwdrivers, chisels and tape measure all in their own little compartments where the Australian wine bottles used to be.

Marlene had tears in her eyes thinking of it.

Coyne made an effort to console her, but said only stupid

things. Rushed into great superlatives of praise and condolence. Tommy will be remembered, Coyne said with great feeling.

Marlene looked surprised. It sounded almost like a threat to her privacy. People like the Nolans didn't want to be remembered. They were afraid of public acknowledgement.

There should be a monument, Coyne said.

What monument? She didn't like the sound of this at all.

He was better than all the rest of them put together, Coyne blubbered. He was suddenly overcome with a great limestone lump in his throat and his lip quivered. Here he was, trying to console Tommy's sister and he ended up crying himself. It was pathetic. Maybe it was all this counselling that had begun to open the floodgates.

Do you want any of his things? she offered. She didn't know what to do with them.

Coyne looked around the room. He was thinking Tommy thoughts. Trying to imagine Tommy's day. As though they were going to be best friends from now on. In retrospect. The great posthumous friendship between the living and the dead. He went home with red rims around his eyes, carrying the wine-carton toolbox.

Coyne was entertaining his emotions. He was getting personally worked up. Involving himself in every local tragedy. Allowing every piece of collective blame to impact straight on his psyche. He was prey to every small downturn in the weather – every little sign of ecological doom. He shouted at the radio, railing against corruption as if it affected him personally. Every change in his country, every sign of progress was an assault on his persona. As though he had become the custodian of purity.

Ms Dunford felt he was overburdened by worldly matters. She continued to try and unlock his mind to find out what made him so vulnerable.

You can't take on the whole world, Pat, she said. You can't solve everything.

She mentioned the possibility of joining group therapy. Perhaps it would be good for him to do something like psycho-drama. Come to terms with his past by re-enacting the traumatic events in front of other people. There was a lot to be said for group sessions.

The first duty is to yourself, Pat. You must enjoy life. That's what we're here for − to have fun.

Coyne was appalled by such a selfish construction of life. That's exactly what the problem was. There was too much fun. People with no other aim in life but gratification. Stuffing themselves.

We're not here to enjoy ourselves, Coyne said.

He would not submit to the tyranny of fun because he was devoted to sorting out the world. His heart went out to all kinds of people he never met. A lot of things had to be put right first before he could start enjoying himself. He was thinking global stuff here as much as local. And what about people in history. How could you forget what happened? How could you turn your back on all that and start tucking in?

Coyne's friend and mentor Fred Metcalf felt it was something more congenital. Coyne had inherited a lament in his head. It was the lonely echo of the Irish language across the Connemara shoreline. He could only think of what was gone, keeping faith with what had disappeared.

Our likes will never be seen again.

It's the sad gene, Fred said. We all have it.

In the blood?

Yes, in the blood. And also not in the blood.

What do you mean?

Whenever they say that people have something in the blood, they're usually talking about exactly the kind of thing that's not in the blood. A nation of people can carry things in various ways, Fred explained. You know the way animals carry their genes from one generation to the next, along biological lines. Well, human evolution is different. We carry genes outside our bodies, through songs and stories. Race memory.

Fred was right. If you thought of Joe Heaney or Caruso – the greatest singers of all time – their genes travelled the world through crackled recordings. Sex was very limited. Samuel Beckett's genes were always more likely to be carried forth into everybody's consciousness through his work than through procreation. These people sent their spiralling messages out like floating dandelion seeds, like parachuting regiments of words drifting across the fields.

Coyne was facing extinction. He remembered being in Connemara as a child. He remembered the sad coastline of Béal an Daingin where he learned Irish. He carried with him a kind of elated loneliness, a great melancholia that sprang from people and the surrounding peninsulas and inlets where he lived.

The all-or-nothing impact of the sea on the shoreline formed his imagination. Every day the landscape changed beyond all recognition when the water receded and left the shore behind. In the morning, the tide could fill the land with great blue and white hope. By afternoon, it migrated almost a mile out from the coast road and the houses, leaving nothing but a vast disillusioned coast where he played alone among the rocks, watching the crabs running sideways at his feet in surprise. Breathing heavily with asthma, with the constant cry of snared prey in his lungs. The high latrine tang of the seaweed in his nostrils, and the thirty-five different Irish names for seaweed in his ears.

The ebb and flow of Coyne's psyche. Standing on the deserted tideline as a boy. A lifeless landscape from which the sea had been drained away and the entire foreshore had been left uncovered, like a great weakness. Limp manes of black seaweed draped across abandoned rocks as though the coast had been struck by a fatal disease. Nothing but the swirling shrieks of curlews and gannets and dogs barking in the distance with deceptive echoes. Everybody had gone off to America and left him behind.

Coyne made another call to Killmurphy, this time from a coin box. Just to keep the pressure on. Early one evening, just when the household was sure to be entering a nice relaxed atmosphere and Killmurphy was probably having his first gin and tonic.

You shouldn't have done it, Killjoy. You and your wife. Nora, isn't it? Living up there in your nice house.

Coyne recalled all the reasons why he was angry at Killjoy. The writ coming in the door. Carmel in tears every day for weeks, thinking it was the end, with disgrace descending all around them. Until her mother finally came to the rescue and put a financial package into place that made Coyne fully subservient and beholden. A failed breadwinner.

Killjoy, you bastard. You'll pay for it. I'll be keeping in touch with you.

The moment had come for Coyne to try and get back with Carmel. It was her birthday. A perfect day for reconciliation. For the past few weeks Coyne had woken up every night talking to her. Dreaming about her rubbing lotion on his back. Dreaming about her eyes. And her laughter.

How had things got this bad?

We belong to each other, Coyne kept saying, like the words of a cheap pop song. He was trapped in the eternal Euro hit of sentimental longing, trying to find some more original way of saying the same thing.

Baby, this is serious! Stop fucking around with my heart, 'cause it's tearing me apart. And don't close the door, because I can't take it any more. You know, love can be so

53

cruel, it will turn me into a mule. Coyne had the fire inside, that cannot be denied.

He hung around the cosmetics department of Brown Thomas trying to choose a gift for her. Something generous but not feckless. Nothing worse than giving her an over-signified birthday present that would be misinterpreted, ultimately, as an audacious advance. He needed something romantic and perfume was by far the most conventional method of approach. To hell with it, Coyne thought, why not buy something expensive?

Trying to make up his mind, he sniffed enough bottles to wipe out an entire colony of laboratory rats. He was suffocating. Any minute, he would be forced to get his inhaler out. Collapse on the floor, gasping, with a little crowd of people standing over him saying: Oh my God. Who was he?

What evolutionary platform had the Irish arrived at now, Coyne thought. Their identity was what they purchased. All around him tills were ringing, credit cards sliding, people making choices with great conviction, while Coyne was stuck at the same counter in a state of perplexed consumer panic. Incapable of making an expedient decision.

The assistant with the orange face mask was doing her best in the circumstances, spraying jets of expensive effluent on her bare arm in polite desperation. The Irishman was becoming very fussy altogether. Used to be a time when they would sneak in with a newspaper, point to the nearest bottle and say: Wrap it up, love. But Coyne was the new breed of Irishman, choosing conscientiously, by way of elimination. After all, it was no longer that straightforward. The tricky territory of postmodern separation, of ex-husband and wife relationships, required some thought. Maybe even an environmental impact study. You couldn't buy any old slurry stink like Eternity, that her mother had probably given her already. Was there nothing called Obnoxious?

Coyne, the great prevaricator. The multi-optional man,

terrorized by choice. Give me the reek of rotting seaweed. Give me haystacks and horse shite. Dunghills and decomposing leaves. The department store stocked every malodorous whiff in history except the one he wanted – the scent Carmel wore when he first met her. He could still remember it clearly. Like fuchsia hedges, laced with cut grass and a subtle background hint of diesel exhaust fumes on a late summer afternoon. Some cheap and ordinary perfume that had long disappeared off the shelves along with his innocence. That was it, the simple romance of the ordinary was no longer available.

Coyne became distracted by a young woman carrying a shoulder bag. He watched as she discreetly sprayed a quick blast of perfume on her wrist, then dropped the bottle into the bag. It was that easy. Only took a second.

Coyne was fascinated. For a man who had spent so much of his life upholding the law, the subversive elegance of this crime suddenly seemed attractive. An act of civil disobedience that confronted his entire devotion to order. Self-service socialism. Coyne had observed her before in the handbag department where he had already spent hours loitering around, sniffing leather, feeling the texture of imitation snakeskin, going through the whole existential breakdown over handbags and finally coming to the decision that it would be an insult to give Carmel a gift like that. I mean, what kind of total gobshite would buy his ex-wife a handbag?

Here! I hope you get mugged, is what it was saying.

Coyne was amazed, as much by his own tolerance as by the sheer audacity of the shoplifter. It seemed easier to steal than to buy. He noticed that she was wearing high-heeled shoes. Strange, he thought, because Coyne's advice to Carmel was always to think of escape. Never make a purchase without assessing the flight implications. Always wear shoes that you can run for your life in.

But it was already too late. The young woman was surrounded by security guards. An older woman in plain clothes approached her, and there was a minor struggle when two security guards took the shoplifter by the arms. One of them speaking into a walkie-talkie.

Coyne told himself not to get involved. You don't need any more complications. Don't jeopardize the compensation claim, like a good man. But he had seen too many of these arrests in the past in the course of his work. Some of them genuine thieves. Some of them just doing it for fun. Others that would break his heart. For the first time, he allowed himself to sympathize with a criminal.

Excuse me, he intervened, before they had a chance to lead her away.

The security personnel looked troubled. He drew the store detective aside and explained that the young woman was not right in the head. Mentally challenged, he said. A ward of court, just out for the day. He apologized for letting her out of his sight. Said he would pay for the goods in question and tried to take the young woman by the arm.

Coyne was proud of himself, thinking all this up on the spot.

The shoplifter assumed a sad, orphaned appearance.

Hold on a minute, one of the security men said. His chest was bursting through his uniform from over-exercise. He had short brown hair, cut neatly into the shape of a square at the back of the neck. A real neck box. In addition to which he possessed a really dangerous set of canine teeth. Coyne returned to the fundamental implications of Darwinism in contemporary Ireland: whether you still needed all that primitive weaponry to bite into a Whopper. He watched the teeth with the fascination of a natural scientist as the security man spoke in his talking clock voice.

I am not at liberty to discuss with you the particulars of this case.

I'll pay, Coyne said, holding out his money.

It is the policy of this store to prosecute offenders, the security man persisted.

Somebody switch off this shaggin' neck box, please.

Coyne had always seen security staff as his allies around the city. His friend, Fred Metcalf was a security guard. They were on the same side of the crime war. But something was happening to Coyne. He suddenly felt like destroying the shop and sending this red-haired primate with the hyena teeth crashing into a rack of Calvin Klein sunglasses. Coyne the great liberator. Of course, he was out of his mind getting into this. He could be charged as an accessory. And what if he made a run for it? They would come after him with video evidence. Coyne would appear on *Crimeline*, like a national celebrity. Have you seen this man? And sure as hell, Carmel's mother would spot it. That's him, she would hiss with glee in her armchair. Delighted to turn him in. Coyne, like an eejit on TV, running towards the exit with a young woman in high heels. That would be the end of Coyne and Carmel.

You're in this together, the sabretoothed security man said.

Coyne became a great persuader. He was on higher ground. Told them he was an off-duty Garda. Paid for the handbag and a bottle of Eternity, as well as some luminous green underwear. Coyne was a little embarrassed by these items being paraded so openly for all to see. The cashier demonstrably folded them at shoulder height. Republican underwear. The wearing of the green!

Her name was Corina. She was Romanian. She offered to buy him a cup of coffee, which, she felt, was the least she could do after him mounting such a daring rescue. Coyne gratefully accepted his reward and they stood in the street for an awkward moment before they walked away in the direction of an Italian café.

The city was changing. There was a greater selection of

cafés in the capital now, and people were beginning to enjoy the notion of diversity as they sat over narcotic cups of coffee, with shopping bags at their feet. They had moved away from the mono-culture of tea and gaudy pink cakes, of rock buns and cream doughnuts with the worm of bright red jam. There was a time when Irish life was concealed with enormous skill behind cups of tea. When the paraphernalia of kettles and teapots provided the stage props of the nation's drama and gave people things to do with their hands while the subtext of ordinary life remained hidden behind the clatter of delph and stirring spoons. Now, things were beginning to look more European. More cappuccino.

Are all Romanians such bad shoplifters? Coyne wanted to know as they sat down.

I never did it before, she said.

Fair enough, it was a promising début, he had to admit. But he wanted to know why she needed to put herself at such risk in the first place. Was shoplifting an act of revolution? His experience told him that there was something else behind this. There was always a cause. A Garda narrative.

I have to make money fast, she said in a burst of anger. Clearly, she objected to this interrogation. Coyne saw defiance in her brown eyes.

Stands to reason, Coyne said. He was also trying to make money fast, through compensation. Who wasn't?

I owe a lot of money, she said. I can't pay it.

She was already working as hard as she could in a fast food restaurant nearby but there was no way that she could meet her debts. She had expected affluence. Streets paved with gold.

Coyne would have suggested some insurance scam. It would make more sense, financially. She would be dealing in larger amounts, with less risk. Maybe a whiplash claim. People were getting rich on car crashes.

Corina began to apologize for her crime. She wasn't

really cut out for it, she hinted. As though Coyne was the host and she was the visitor who had been caught pilfering the silver cutlery. Her momentary remorse allowed Coyne to ask more questions, and slowly she revealed how she had come to Ireland. He got the information in small increments – the journey by sea, the long hours locked inside a cabin.

Christ, he thought. These were the Blasket Islanders coming back. The tide of emigration was turning. Here they were, the first of them – thousands who had fled poverty and were now returning at last.

You're coming back, he said.

She didn't understand this enigmatic shift of gear in Coyne's attitude. He was speaking with great feeling now. Looking at her through watery eyes.

The islanders, he said.

Corina shook her head and smiled at this complete misunderstanding. It had nothing to do with any language barrier either, because the Romanians were the best linguists in the world, and she had already picked up a number of key Dublin colloquial phrases, such as I'm broke. I'm skinned. Altogether!

She had difficulty understanding what Coyne was saying now. He was entertaining his emotions again. He wanted to help her, give her money. Then he decided to write down his phone number for her. But she looked at him accusingly. Pushed the piece of paper away.

What do you want?

If you're in trouble, he offered.

I'm going to split, she said. This had obviously gone too far. She got up from her seat. I have to meet somebody, she said. She pushed the handbag and its contents into Coyne's lap. Thanked him and walked away from the table, leaving Coyne behind, looking up with a helpless expression of rejected kindness.

Wait, he said. I'm serious. If you're stuck?

He went running after her through the café. Knocking his own chair over with a great clack of undignified urgency as he chased her with the shopping bag in his hand.

The Anchor Bar, he said.

But it sounded sad, like he was looking for a favour from her in return for the rescue. She turned around and squared up to him. Looked as though she was going to punch him. She didn't trust Coyne's hospitality any more. Didn't need his help. Like she was saying: I can look after myself, you know. I don't need a man to sort things out for me. Then she was gone. And Coyne went back to his seat and sat down.

Mongi O Doherty was such a dedicated capitalist that he perceived cash as an awkward medium, an obstacle to the flow of capital. The physical collection of money was a nuisance which slowed down the whole process of amassing wealth. The trend was towards the virtual transactions of credit cards, to ease the resistance and make the concept of money more spiritual. Payments should be like prayers. Decades of the rosary. Novenas. In God we trust! Cash was a grubby, secular substance which he didn't like to handle personally.

Corina first had to pay her money over to a third party in a city pub. It was a lodgement, so to speak. After which a phone call was made on a mobile phone, and she was then instructed to go to another specified pub to meet Mongi O Doherty himself. An audience with the money Buddha.

The instalment was disappointing, is what he was there to tell her. He appreciated the sight of hard currency coming into his possession, but the amount was too small, that's all.

I mean, how do you expect any of your ex-Soviet countries ever to integrate fully into Europe if you can't speed up the rate of repayments?

We're doing our best, Corina said.

Mongi forced himself to be pleasant and courteous. He

had an idea that might help her. A kind of Marshall Plan, if you like, that would enable her to make better use of her natural resources and generate income more rapidly. He bought her a drink, which she tried to decline, looking at the daiquiri with the cherry and the plastic sabre with some amusement. If only this could be converted back into money to pay off more of her debt.

Initially Mongi was offended by her lack of gratitude. He explained that sometimes it was good to look like you had money. Money had a sacred element that gave off an aura. It made people 'holy', or cool. As a former moneylender, he was in a position to tell her that the appearance of wealth was often enough to achieve paradise.

Corina looked at Mongi's dress code to see if it matched the philosophy. He wore shiny blue tracksuit bottoms with white stripes down the side of the leg, and a T-shirt with sleek greyhounds running at great speed across his chest. He wore white socks and black slip-on shoes.

I have some contacts who could point you in the right direction, he said. You could buy some plenary indulgences, if you get my drift.

Indulgences? Corina was listening. Sipping poison.

It doesn't need to be that difficult, Mongi said, looking her up and down. If you put on a bit of make-up. Rob some decent clothes. I know people in that line of business who could see you right.

What are you talking about?

You have a great body, he said at last. You know what I'm saying. You could use it.

Dracu, she said, getting up to leave.

Mongi put a firm hand on her arm. There were debts to be paid, he insisted. A boat trip on a luxury trawler, with cabin accommodation. He needed a quick repayment schedule. His patience was running out.

I'm not doing purgatory for you, he said.

It was like the old days. Carmel's birthday and everybody sitting around the table in the happy Irish home. Coyne and Jimmy back in the bosom of the family and Carmel's mother bringing out the cake that looked like a UFO with a forest of lit candles on top. It was Carmel's idea to bring everyone together for occasions like this. Even if they were separated, there were some essential family rituals that need not be lost.

Mrs Gogarty was sceptical. Coyne noticed that she had started using the word 'actually' all the time. It was a theatrical distancing technique, and Coyne wanted to call her Mrs Actually, only that he was on his best behaviour and didn't want to squander the privilege of being allowed to attend the party. Coyne had a few drinks before he arrived. Heavy smell of alcohol all over the birthday cake.

Jennifer and Nuala were the only ones who were misbehaving. Fighting among themselves, calling each other bitch and cow over some clothes they had borrowed and not given back, until Mrs Gogarty said she'd had enough. This was Carmel's birthday. They should all respect that.

Carmel was stupefied by Coyne's gift. A real leather shoulder bag and a bottle of Eternity inside. How did you know, Pat? she exclaimed. She had nearly run out of perfume. And it was her favourite too.

Jennifer and Nuala took it off her and sprayed themselves immediately. The air was thick already.

While they were occupied with the scent, Carmel put her hand into the bag and took out the green underwear. Looked at it for a moment in disbelief, then pushed it back quickly, out of sight. Mrs Actually missed nothing. She had seen the outrageous, ex-husband sexual proposal that was contained in this gift. Generosity is a form of conquest, she always maintained.

You shouldn't have, Carmel said, holding up the bag and feeling the leather. It's too generous, Pat.

I'll be getting compensation, Coyne blubbered.

She kissed him dutifully. A courtesy kiss. Cheek to cheek, with a large slice of air in between, and Mrs Actually monitoring the whole thing at close range like a referee in a boxing ring. Ready to shout 'break' and separate the contestants.

Coyne was chuffed with himself. So much so that he started cracking jokes with Jennifer and Nuala. Taking the sweeping brush and pretending to sweep the kitchen floor. Then helping to carry cups and dishes out to the kitchen until Mrs Actually blocked his way, taking things out of his hands.

Mrs Gogarty, they should name a drink after you, he said. She gave him a fierce look and spun around on her hind legs.

This is the way things should be again, Coyne thought. Of course it was all his fault in the first place. He was the first to admit it. His drinking. His fooling around. His moods. But he was ready to go straight over that waterfall of domestic bliss as he watched Carmel laughing as she used to in the old days. He could not see why they had ever separated.

It's insane, Carmel, he wanted to shout.

Despite all the good will, Coyne could not persuade Carmel to go to the pub with him. Take one step inside a public bar with that man, and you'll never come out, Mrs Gogarty warned. Actually, taking one step in any direction with that man is a fatal mistake.

Carmel didn't know how she could allow herself to go out with her ex-husband on her birthday. It would mean that she had nobody else in her life and was still depending on Coyne for emotional partnership. It was for the sake of the children, she told herself. And in some respects she took pity on Coyne since the fire. Was it possible that his victim-hero status was slowly winning her over? She considered the expensive gifts he had bought for her. The least she could do was go for a walk with him. But she was not ready to give up her independence to be seen in some squalid pub.

Instead she suggested Irish dancing. I need a partner, she said.

Coyne didn't catch the irony.

You've had bad experiences with Irish dancing, Carmel.

She was willing to put it all behind her. Everybody is into it now, she said. There was a set-dancing revival club in every suburb, she added with great enthusiasm.

Riverfluke, in other words, Coyne muttered. People hopping around to *The Stacks of Barley*.

Carmel was keen to relive her childhood. She had won a lot of medals doing Tara Brooch dancing as a little girl. A cross between show jumping and the goosestep.

The country is changing, she said. People are proud of their heritage. It will be good for your chest as well.

Irish dancing was no way to repair your lungs, or your marriage, Coyne thought. But what could he do? He agreed to join her, even just to carry out a discreet little quality control check on this latest revival. He was the custodian of heritage. Coyne had learned a few steps himself when he was a young lad. Of course, he could have done with another drink beforehand, just to work up the courage. With enough drink he might even have felt he was rejoining society. Getting into the new Ireland.

But it was too much to expect. Coyne was off on his own ideological counter-attack.

For fucksake, he muttered when he saw the incompetence of the dancers. What a graceless pack of heifers.

Pat, come on. Just get into it, she said. You'll love it.

Coyne waited on the sidelines. What was going on here? These people didn't know the difference between Irish dancing and a haka. A woman wobbled past him with a low-cut dress, breasts churning around like she was making

64

butter. Tina Turner gyrating on the Cliffs of Moher. A man stomping around with her like a cowboy, kicking dust and waltzing on bandy legs, like he'd been sitting on a horse all day. Coyne wanted to go up to him and give him a clout on the back of the head. Give that up. Dance properly. Stop moving your neck, you blackguard. And stop that pelvic thrusting, all of you. That's got nothing to do with Irish dancing.

Don't be such a purist, Carmel said. It's all evolving.

Look at them wiggling, Coyne said in despair, pointing directly at the woman shaking her fuselage. He watched the new hip movements with great alarm. Where was the subtle introspection of Irish culture? The secrecy? The provocative understatement?

You're stuck in the past, Carmel said.

This is all wrong, Coyne raged.

As far as he was concerned, it had everything to do with the past. Irish dancing had its own unique swing. It was a triumph of control, with none of this cheap Riverfluke grandeur. How could you hope to merge humility with tacky exhibitionism? It was a cultural contradiction in terms, like a convertible Ferrari with a thatched roof. Where was the grace that made old women in Connemara look like young girls with their lightfooted dignity?

Coyne had lost it. The one chance he had of getting back with Carmel was about to be aimlessly thrown away on this primitive argument. He was determined to show these people what Irish dancing was about. An exhibition they would not forget. He took a puff on his inhaler and leapt out like an okapi. Like he had fallen out of the sky. With stunning poise. His shoulders twitching in time to the music, a look of abject dementia in his open eyes, and his self-raising hair standing up on his head with great vigour. He moved as steadily as a ship. Only the heel every now and again slamming down on the wooden floor, punctuating the beat with an emphatic bang as he swung Carmel around the dance floor. He was back in the Aran Islands, dancing in the Kilronan Hall, with the generator purring outside.

But as usual, Coyne went too far. People looked up in shock. Suburban novices, frightened by the sheer authenticity of his movements. They left a big gap of respect around him. Coyne the mountainy man, as cold and passionate as the dawn, yahooing and leaving casualties all around him. Swinging the wiggle out of Tina Turner and sending her practically into orbit. Until she was so seasick that she had to sit down with her head between her legs. White in the face. And her husband holding out a glass of water towards her.

Carmel was furious as she dragged Coyne outside. He was a bogman. Dancing was all about courtesy. Not some contest of strength.

Go back to aerobics, he shouted over his shoulder. You pack of flatfooted gobshites.

And then outside the hall, Coyne started coughing like he was going to die before he could justify his crusading intervention. Stood there with his hand against the wall for a clear ten minutes, rasping and dragging up a string of emerald green rosary beads which he spat on the ground outside like a warning to all dancers.

Take the wiggle out of Irish dancing!

Carmel drove home in silence. Couldn't wait to get rid of him. Coyne had definitely blown it this time. It was the end all right. Though when she pulled up outside his flat, he tried to cling on to some hope of a reunion. Refused to get out of the car and asked her straight out if she wanted to come inside for a cup of coffee. He still had a lot to say about Irish culture.

The idea of it. She looked astonished. *And I'd like to know where – you got the notion*, is what she was saying with her eyes. Trying to make a pass at your ex-wife, for Godsake.

I've got to go, she said.

It's you and me, Carmel, he said with another gust of

passion, as if he'd met her for a tryst. We're inextricably linked.

She pushed him out of the car. Alarmed. Drove away and left him standing.

We're inextricably linked, he repeated to the empty street.

Coyne's attitude to women needed urgent exploration. Ms Dunford thought he was not only psychotic but dangerously unbalanced. He was in love with Carmel but he couldn't take his mind off women in general for more than a minute at a time. He admitted to having an uncontrollable fetish about tartan skirts, bra straps and knicker lines.

His relationship with women was more like a contest. Some big gender warfare, brought on perhaps by the way he was educated in single-sex schools, and the way the men and women gathered on opposite sides of the dancehalls in Béal an Daingin and in the Aran Islands. Or the men gathered in groups together outside Mass. And men together in the pub. It simplified everything into a clearly defined go-get-them role, but also left him without a vocabulary to deal with women, except as a lover. Love was easy. Talking was hard.

Why did you leave your wife?

I don't really know, he said.

Was it freedom? Some need to liberate yourself?

Coyne resented the question. This was like a mental grope. Scraping at his innermost secrets. He protected himself, speaking in riddles. She had identified the problem, something awry in the nature of men; some deep, ongoing crisis that they carried around with them all the time, even when they looked happy and amused and well adjusted. Coyne was restless. He could not trust himself.

I'm not in control, he said. I never was.

You need control?

I just never know where I stand, that's all.

While Coyne was living with Carmel, he wanted to get away. Now he couldn't wait to get back with her. Maybe there was some profound contradiction in the male psyche that could never be reconciled, except through the active pursuit of desires – women, goals, music, football. Men like Coyne were never stationary. They were like mackerel, without the air-bag necessary to maintain a steady place in the water. They were forced to keep moving all the time, chasing around the pelagic depths of the ocean at forty kilometres an hour, all day and all night, unable to stay still for any length of time. Coyne the restless mackerel, like a channel surfer's nightmare: obsessed with what he was missing.

You should join one of those men's groups, Ms Dunford advised.

What?

A lot of men are starting to meet and discuss their problems these days.

What the hell was she on about? No way was he going to join up with some bunch of wackos in short trousers talking about their feelings and getting in touch with their instincts. Out there in some forest with bow and arrows, dancing around the campfire, chanting and bawling like lost elks. Primordial men, getting it all off their chests.

In any case, what Coyne wanted could never really be discussed out in the open without destroying it. There would always be something dark and unspeakable about his desires, some innate contradiction. Coyne was a walking paradox.

Sergeant Corrigan was trying to expand his investigation. He was casting a wider net, so to speak, and the biblical metaphor was appropriate since he had begun to investigate the entire fishing community. He went through every trawler. Spoke to skippers and sailors, some of whom had been asleep below deck when Tommy Nolan met his death. They must have heard something.

He encountered a conspiracy of ignorance. Empty nets. Fish-head silence.

Normally Sergeant Corrigan was more inclined to employ DIY metaphors. He was one of those who never stopped improving things. A true handyman. Every available minute off duty was spent sawing and drilling. At the weekend, he wandered around his home, measuring everything in sight.

He had come down one morning early to do a few measurements at the harbour. As far as most of the fishing people were concerned, Corrigan should stay at home and measure his own mickey. They were seriously pissed off with this DIY stuff. Watched with contempt as Corrigan climbed down the side of trawlers, measuring the gap between boats and the quay. The angle of fall. The slack of mooring ropes.

Sergeant Corrigan seemed to concentrate on skipper Martin Davis.

Is the tide coming in or going out? he asked.

Martin Davis was a busy man, and if the sergeant had nothing more serious in mind, he would like to get on with his work. Corrigan got a bit testy. He didn't like to be rushed on his DIY jobs. He was the type of man who asked questions a second time if he didn't get an answer. He belonged to the measure-twice-cut-once persuasion.

You facilitated Tommy's funeral, he said accusingly. You helped dispose of the ashes.

Tommy did a few jobs for me, Davis answered with a hint of genuine respect for the dead. I was indebted to him. He was a great guy.

But Corrigan was never going to be happy with the answer. He was there to measure things again and again. Maybe everything was not quite fish fingers at the harbour, he thought.

The skipper squinted against the sun. The glare reflecting across the surface of the harbour was suddenly too much for him. Besides, Martin Davis was getting very irritated at being mistaken for a plank of timber. Sergeant Corrigan had a pencil behind his ear and looked at Martin Davis as though he could build shelves on his face.

From there, Sergeant Corrigan went straight on to the Haven nursing home where he interviewed Jimmy Coyne again. Another vital piece of information had emerged – a discrepancy, if you like, between Jimmy's version of events and his friend Gussy's. Of course, it had to be taken into consideration that they were both drunk and stoned on the night in question. Neither of them was reliable. The Sergeant was trying to work out why Jimmy had stayed at the harbour after Gussy went home.

I don't know, Jimmy said. I fell asleep.

A real schoolboy answer, Corrigan thought. This time he found Jimmy's behaviour strange. A little distant. Not quite in touch with reality. He formed the opinion that Jimmy was either very guilty, or else he had taken some kind of narcotic substance that prevented him from thinking clearly and giving rational answers. It was like talking to somebody with senile dementia.

Did you encounter Tommy Nolan?

You're in the vestibule, Jimmy said.

What's that supposed to mean?

Jimmy shrugged as though he didn't know what he meant himself.

Look, I can take you into the station if you like, Corrigan threatened.

They quickly reached a kind of stalemate in the reception room of the Haven. It was clear that Corrigan had nothing more than suspicion on his side. Just a gut feeling. Hunch science. They sat looking at the calendar depicting a smiling over-seventies couple jogging through a forest and a schnauzer running beside them, trying hard to keep up. Lactulose! Like clockwork! Corrigan's mouth had gone into the silent whistle formation. Like he could have done with a spoonful of lactulose himself.

Jimmy Coyne was in love. At the old people's home, surrounded by all that morbidity and decline, he discovered a great longing for life. He followed Nurse Boland around wherever he could. He brushed against her accidentally and she punched him back, accidentally. They slagged each other all the time and brightened up the mausoleum wards, as she called them. The age difference was meaningless and Jimmy told the old people he loved her. For the inhabitants of the home it was like a live soap opera unfolding in front of their eyes.

The nuns who administered the nursing home felt that Jimmy was a deeply caring person. He understood the needs of these people, the casualties of time clinging on to life day by day. Sad old people and happy old people, holding on to their memories, encouraged by visits from their relatives. He understood the frustration of age and observed how Mrs Broadbent would grope for an hour or more, trying to find a mini-torch that she kept under her pillow. Others were fumbling around with their memory. Asking what time it was. Whether they'd had their breakfast yet when it was already time to go to bed.

One of the patients, Mr Grogan, always had trouble putting his trousers on. A former high-ranking member of the Civil Service, he was still determined to fend for himself but came down to Mass every second day with some garment inside out. Once Jimmy found him in his room, late in the evening, with one foot in his jacket sleeve.

But this was nothing when compared to the bodily failures which characterized this home. The entire place was held together by ointments and eye drops, baby oil and disinfectant. Not to mention slow-releasing morphine. Key words that had entered into Jimmy's vocabulary. The old people were infants at the latter end of the arc, losing words. Saying Ma Ma and Da Da for the last time, their skills reducing by the day. Jimmy soon got to know their smells: Fish, sardines, leather and banana. He knew the pungent stench of their incontinence sheets, the blend of perished rubber and urine. But he also knew the softness of old people. The frailty of their bones. The beauty in their wrinkled folds of flesh. He helped them to the bathroom. He helped Nurse Irene to wash them. Lifted them in and out of the bath.

Jimmy loved the squeaking sound when Nurse Boland put on the rubber gloves. Every day he helped her with fresh sheets and pillowcases. Most of the time, he hindered her. Playing games and trying to annoy her; throwing water at her until she picked up a stick belonging to one of the old people and started chasing after him, through the rooms, across the beds and along the corridor. Nurse Boland at last managing to whack Jimmy on the backside and extracting a yelp of pain and helpless laughter out of him.

The shocking speed of their games made the old people dizzy. They could see what was coming, as though this romance was being played out for them vicariously. And one day, like a leap of evolution, the exhibition took a new twist. While Nurse Boland stood there with her rubber gloves in the air and her back to a row of nodding patients in their wheelchairs, Jimmy lifted her uniform and showed all the old men and women Nurse Boland's underwear. Just a quick semi-consensual glimpse which sent them all nodding into infinity.

Nurse Boland's white lace underwear for all to see. She turned around but Jimmy was already on the run, driving a wheelchair at high speed down the corridor. Looking back at the last minute to see Nurse Boland with her rubber gloves in the air, looking like a nuclear physicist with a burning smile on her face. I'll get you!

Coyne was fighting with everyone these days. His father had come from Cork, the rebel county, the part of Ireland perhaps best known for its noble tradition of insurgency. Michael Collins country. But what use was all that rebel greatness now? What could you do in times of advanced peace and prosperity with the faculties of rebellion, nurtured over centuries? It was like an overactive immune response that was long obsolete.

He had a brief altercation with Martin Davis outside the Anchor Bar one night. As the skipper came out and he was going in, he allowed his suspicions to reach the surface.

You're not doing much fishing these days, Captain.

Bud focain asail, Martin Davis responded, walking away.

So the skipper was a garlic speaker, Coyne thought. Delighted with the chance to show off his links with the past, Coyne took up the challenge. Struck back with his own range of expletives, shouting down the street after him, like he was performing in some outdoor pageant. *Poll séidigh!*

Diúg mo bhud, a mhac!, the skipper said over his shoulder.

A hot battle of insults as they vilified each other outside the Anchor Bar in the mother tongue. It drew respect and admiration, as though they belonged to an elite little club of Irish speakers who would greet each other in the pub every night from now on with this barbaric invective.

Coyne was besieged by the past. All the ghosts were coming back to stalk him. One day he ran almost straight into Mr Killmurphy.

Maybe the phone calls were working, because Killmurphy seemed to give Coyne a very serious and inquisitive look when they saw each other on the seafront. Coyne was walking towards the gentlemen's bathing spot. Forty foot gentlemen only. Not for a swim or anything healthy like that. Just to have a look. And who does he see only Killjoy?

He hadn't laid eyes on him for years. Assumed he must

73

have moved to a different branch, because Coyne was dealing with a younger manager now. But the sight of Killjoy brought out all the old animosity. The basilisk-eyed bank manager. Staring at him. For a moment, it even looked like Killjoy was going to come over to Coyne and talk to him; perhaps start accusing him of sabotaging his garden.

The past was full of atrocities.

Coyne threw him a look of triumph. It was a moment of moral superiority when Coyne remembered exactly why he had gone to such extremes. The siege mentality.

Yes, Killjoy, you're absolutely right. It's me. Coyne the patio terrorist.

Coyne still had friends in the force. He was trying to find some way of getting his hands on Tommy Nolan's post-mortem report. People owed him favours all over the place, but there was nobody around who would risk their neck on that one, let alone know how to go about getting it in the first place. Leaking out a pathology report was a tricky one, so Coyne had to ask Fred Metcalf. He was the only contact who could deliver when it came down to the wire. Even though Fred was retired now and living alone, he still had important connections in the detective branch.

It was a matter of life and death, Coyne explained. He wouldn't be asking, if it wasn't. And Coyne swore that he would never ask another favour as long as he lived.

I'll have to twist a few arms on that one, Fred said. It wasn't that he didn't trust Coyne. It was just a bit of trouble getting possession of documents like that. He was really looking for a good reason, that's all.

Coyne had brought him a box of Kentucky Fried Chicken. His favourite.

Tommy Nolan was a friend, Coyne said.

Coyne gave no further explanation. He sat down and

drank tea. Watched Fred put the chicken meal away for later and eat a half-dozen pink Mikado biscuits instead.

Fred was an old man now. He was slow, and struggled with the simplest of tasks. He had a scratching disease that drove him insane at times, sitting in his armchair all day trying to keep calm. If he was a dog, Fred explained once to Coyne, he'd have a lampshade around his neck to stop him scratching. Coyne took pity on him and occasionally thought he would end up like Fred himself, sitting in front of the TV all day, eating biscuits and scratching.

Coyne had promised to bring his two daughters out. Took them into town one afternoon because they wanted to get their bellybuttons pierced. How could he argue with them. He just had to make sure it was all cleared with Carmel and Mrs Gogarty first.

The girls had reached an accommodation over who was going to do what piercing. They agreed that Jennifer was going to get her bellybutton done, and Nuala was going to get her nose pierced. Coyne was utterly malleable. In situations like this, they could walk over him. He went along with personal freedom of choice. If his daughter wanted to put in an extra nostril in her nose, then he couldn't stop her. Even agreed to pay for it.

But things were different when they got into the Body Culture store: a dark little studio with pictures of mutilated victims all over the walls.

The owner came out from behind a curtain, stooped with the ton of steel hanging off his face. There was a hole in his earlobe the size of a large coin. His arms were covered in tattoos, blurred snakes and daggers which had stretched with age and elongated flabbiness. The girls began to get a little nervous and self-conscious.

Coyne told the man he wanted a nose and a bellybutton job. Pointed at his daughters.

The piercer produced a disclaimer agreement and

explained that the piercing wounds might take months to heal. And if anything went wrong, if there were any medical complications later on, he could take no responsibility. It looked as though Mr Body Culture himself was beginning to regret each one of his own mutilations.

Coyne insisted. On behalf of Nuala and Jennifer, he was ready to sign the form. Until one of them began to get worried.

I don't want to, Nuala said, and the whole thing began to go into reverse. The great confidence which they had worked on for weeks slipped away. It was the picture of pierced nipples on the wall that got them. They left the dark little torture studio in a hurry.

Jennifer and Nuala were silent, walking with their dad through the warm sunlit Dublin streets. Off along Grafton Street, not knowing what to say any more because their great mission was abandoned. Coyne could see they were disappointed. They were still only children. Though they were too old to be told stories, he was still able to spin a kind of fantasy for them. He bought them clothes. Bracelets and eye make-up. Helped them feel better. Took them in for cakes and cappuccino.

He got the bus back and walked with them as far as the gate of his old home. Nuala asked him to come inside. He was reluctant at first, but how could he refuse? His youngest daughter's mind had not yet understood the partition in her parents' life and still saw them as one entity. Still saw her father as the man who had sat at the end of the bed telling stories.

Carmel was out at the time, so Coyne decided to go inside briefly. What harm was it to behave like a real father. To go and examine Nuala's school project on the Dalai Lama. Coyne felt a strange sensation of regained memory as he climbed the stairs, as though he had dropped back in time. He was bewildered by his old home. Sat for a while admiring Nuala's work, asking questions, adding things that he knew about the subject.

What's that for? Coyne asked suddenly, when he noticed a white line drawn with chalk on the carpet.

The peace line, Nuala said.

The girls looked at each other and began to explain how they had drawn a demarcation line in the middle of the room, dividing it into halves, one for Nuala, the other for Jennifer. A virtually invisible boundary across which they were not allowed to step. While Coyne was in the room on his rare visit, they suddenly struck an unspoken truce which allowed them to ignore the normal rules of engagement. Coyne the great peace envoy.

When they had shown their father everything, and it was time for Coyne to leave again, they suddenly became very hospitable. Urging him to stay for a while longer, they offered him tea and went downstairs to put the kettle on. Get the biscuits out.

Coyne was on his way down after them when he caught a glimpse of his own former bedroom. He stood on the landing for a moment, tempted to take a look inside.

Why not?

While the girls were busy downstairs, he stood in Carmel's bedroom, towering over the bed he had slept in. He looked at the curtains and the window where he had so often stood at night looking out at the nocturnal golfer next door. Everything was so seductively familiar that it began to wash over him until he felt that nothing had changed, a ghost-like figure in his own life.

Carmel's paintings were on the walls. Along the vanity desk, her painted stones which reminded him of one of the last arguments they had. It drove Coyne mad that she had begun to make use of stones from the shore. How could you possibly hope to improve them? They had an authentic seashore look; an integrity that had taken millions of years of erosion to achieve until she started mutilating them with silly little dots and faces. Tarting them up with zigzag colours. Systematically eliminating the last unspoiled link to prehistoric purity.

On the bed there was a big white teddy bear that Carmel had won in a raffle at one of the local shops on Valentine's Day. On the duvet were more stones. Not painted stones this time, but stones in their original beauty which Carmel had collected for their healing qualities. I want to touch people, she had once said. My talent is in giving. She had selected these stones for their shapes and their beneficial potential. They contained infinity, polished and smoothed by time. Lying on the side of the bed, where he had once slept, he now saw a variety of stones and pebbles, some grey with white markings, some white, one with what looked like a planetary ring. Another stone that she had picked up from the tunnelling workers – a white granite ball like an ostrich egg, excavated from the big new sewerage tunnel, deep under Dublin Bay.

Coyne sat at the edge of the bed. The stones rolled together with the click of pool balls. He was looking at the sun-heated shoreline on the bed, transfixed as if sitting on a remote strand, with the red sunset of a bedside lamp going down on the horizon. Carmel like a topless sunbather, sitting at the edge of the water, smiling. Sheets and duvet lapping around her knees. A handprint on the sand where she was propped on one long sloping arm, with a dimple above her elbow, the other hand toying with the stones. Shifting them around self-consciously with her fingers. He imagined her taking one of the smallest polished pebbles, red in the glow of the sun, and placing it against one of her breasts.

Coyne reached out and picked up a stone – cool at first, then warm in his hand. It was the one with the white Saturn ring. It fitted perfectly into his cupped palm, like a sculpted breast. He felt the weight of it, threw it in the air a little and caught it again with a satisfying smack. He liked this stone and wanted to keep it. To steal it from her and hide it in his own flat, like a secret possession, a memory, a physical souvenir of Carmel. He put it in his pocket and went back downstairs, triumph and guilt on equal rank as he felt the stone against his leg.

The following day, Coyne collected the post-mortem report on Tommy Nolan: the last details on a posthumous friend. At a glance, he could see references pertaining to a head injury. Pages and pages, all about the one injury alone. But he closed the document again because it would be wrong to read it on the bus, like a copy of the *Star* newspaper. Reading about Tommy's death as if it was a soccer report.

He waited till he got back to the flat. Decided to have lunch first, though he was not really hungry. Food was more like a rite of passage that marked the separation of one part of the day from another. He put the report on the kitchen table, hung his jacket around the shoulders of a chair and began to prepare some eggs.

Coyne was inefficient in the kitchen. He switched the cooker on too soon and allowed the blue flame to hiss away urgently while he fumbled around in the fridge getting out the eggs. He found a bowl and cracked one of the eggs against the rim, not vigorously enough, so that the egg still held together and Coyne had to force it open, getting egg all over his thumb in the process.

Normally, Carmel would have taken over at this point. Come here, give it to me – I can't bear to watch this! Either that or her mother Mrs Actually would have become involved and Coyne would have found himself barred from the kitchen. But he was taking control of his own food now. The second egg cracked with far too much force and Coyne spent more time picking out bits of shell. Then he whisked the egg and started enjoying the rhythm.

The timing was wrong. He went back to the fridge more than three times. First for butter, then for milk, then for a scallion. The toast was done long before the scrambled egg was started. He cut the toast into triangles, just as Carmel would have done, but then forgot to make the tea. And when he finally sat down to eat his lunch, he had lost his appetite. Somehow, it was the achievement of producing the meal that mattered more than any physical need. He ate the first few forkfuls voraciously, like a starving man, chewing on the crisp bread and the soft, salty egg. Sipping the tea. Looking at the brown envelope containing the post-mortem report.

Coyne had become a furtive eater. He looked around as he ate. He crossed his legs and began to swing his foot in and out. He was uncomfortable with himself. Instead of feeling gratification and calmness, his mind frequently made the lateral jump to something distasteful, as though disgust had become the most prominent, overstated instinct of self-preservation. At moments when he sat down to eat his meal, he would suddenly think of the worst possible image. Faeces. Violence. Blood. Pictures of psoriasis. Worms emerging from a wound. A drowned dog he had seen floating just beneath the surface of the water in the harbour, with an orange rope around its neck, eyes gone white. A chain reaction of ugliness asserted itself in his mind every time he sat down to his food. His stomach churned in revolt, and he was already pushing the plate away.

Coyne had begun to develop a serious eating disorder, according to his psychologist. Perhaps he was experiencing some belated race memory. She didn't want to overemphasize it for fear of fuelling the problem. Coyne was now losing his appetite during the day, and then waking up in the middle of the night with a raging hunger. Ms Dunford tried to minimize it by blaming the years of shift work and bad dietary habits in the Gardai.

A feeling of guilt made it impossible for him to celebrate food in the normal way. There was no word for *bon appetit* in Irish. There was no way of rejoicing in bounty. No formal language, no vocabulary with which to encourage people to eat, except perhaps for some of the more crass expressions that had emerged more recently, like dig in! Eating remained a clandestine thing, and the only traditional phrase Coyne could remember in connection with food was a vicious, begrudging one to do with choking. All manner of things, even entirely unrelated to food, were brought under that vicious curse.

Go dtachtfaidh sé thú! May it choke you!

Besides, Irish cuisine had a long way to go. They had started experimenting with things like black pudding, but the Irish would basically eat anything as long as it was dead and came with french fries. They were either starving or stuffed. And they would never go so far as to prefer food to singing. If it came down to the straight Pepsi challenge between *moules marinière* and *The Town That I Loved So Well* – no contest.

Sergeant Corrigan had his lunch at the Marine Hotel. It was the main meal of the day for him. Carvery lunch in the lounge. Chefs in white hats and red faces behind a self-service counter. Corrigan was not interested in the smoked cod pie or the *boeuf bourguignon*, so he opted for the bacon and cabbage with potatoes in their jackets. Just what he loved.

Corrigan was accompanied by a younger colleague who chose the *bourguignon*. The chef wiped his hands on a blue and white checquered apron before handling the food. Sharpened a short carving knife with a musical interlude before cutting fresh slices of bacon. Smiled and gave the sergeant extra, knowing that he was in the force. Corrigan rubbed his hands in anticipation.

The Marine carvery had the atmosphere of a sanctuary. Plate sounds and cutlery clash. The low hum of monotone voices: a rising babble of sufficiency. Corrigan and his colleague sat at a round table in silence. For them, food was still of such primary importance that a curfew prevailed. Until they crossed the hunger threshold they could not really afford to get into any serious conversation.

How are the wardrobes coming on? his colleague attempted.

Fine, Corrigan said, and normally he would have been only too delighted to start talking about the cult of home improvement. Every screw, every measurement, every tricky corner. His new black ash veneer built-in wardrobes with tinted mirrors were a matter of great pride. But this was not the time for it.

Corrigan opened the buttons on his jacket and sat leaning forward, knees apart on either side of the round table. One of his feet curled round the leg of his chair for support. Red napkin on his right thigh like a piper's patch as he peeled one of the potatoes. The noble spud. Big as a lumper. He picked it up in his hand and stripped away the freckled skin with meticulous care, catching it between thumb and knife and exposing the bright and steaming pulp underneath. There was a slight frown on his forehead and a barely concealed smile on his face as he concentrated on this intimate task. He respected the potato and seemed to be talking to it all along. Come on, take your jacket off now, like a good lad. You're far too hot. He undressed it quickly, juggling the hot core around on a tripod of his fingers until he had finished and dropped it gently on to the plate, right beside the cabbage. Jacket folded away neatly on a side plate. Then he plunged the knife into the centre and the yellow-white, powdery landfalls of flesh fell apart. Steam bursting up from the scalding interior. Butter melting into a golden pool.

He ate with gusto and possessed excellent food management skills. He cut a triangle of pink bacon, anointed it with a touch of mustard and moved his torso forward so that his head came to meet the fork. Again and again, this repeated welcoming motion. Bowing to the bacon. Following it up with a forkful of cabbage and potato. He held the knife like a fountain pen, deftly levering a bale of cabbage on to the fork and bonding it temporarily with the adhesive potato mash, before moving his body forward again to meet the oncoming food.

The potato was still too hot, so he whistled a bit to cool it down. Then he remembered to drink his cordial, before starting the same routine again. His eating was carried out in a series of well organized clearing operations. Demolition and disposal. Keeping an eye on the custard trifle to follow.

His eyes were in fact semi-glazed. He looked out the window towards the seafront but failed to see the band of blue water. He half noticed people coming and going. But his eyes stopped seeking information. His vision was impaired. Women and men could have danced naked on the other side of the room. He was virtually blind to anything further away than two feet around him. A kind of voluntary blindness. As if there was an area cordoned off with crime scene tape, beyond which everything was a watery blur.

John McCurtain had lunch at the Anchor Bar. It was as convenient as anywhere else. He intended to make a right pig of himself. He was starving and Kelly's did a great sandwich.

Port and Docks! That's what McCurtain worked at. Nobody ever knew what exactly that meant, or what kind of duties he performed. It could have been anything from sweeping the offices to designing lighthouses. It didn't seem to matter much. The Port and Docks board was a kind of vocation that embraced a great number of men and women under a cloak of respectability.

McCurtain walked into the Anchor and slapped the *Star* newspaper on the counter. Sat up on the stool and started reading the front page. Ordered a ham and cheese toasted sandwich with relish. An American touch. He also asked for onion rings. The truth lay in between the slices of a sandwich at the Anchor Bar.

It was more like a meal, both in price and handling. Not the kind of sandwich you could hold in one hand while you had a pint in the other. It was a knife and fork situation, with thick, generous rivers of relish running like lava out from between the slices. McCurtain lashed into it. Cut smartly with a downward motion of his elbow, and a look of disdain on his face which seemed to imply that he actually reviled what he was about to eat and enjoy. His nose was curled up. Mouth shaped into a grin. And his eyes leering at the food like a voyeur.

He sat up straight, inhaling deeply as he chewed and stared at the topless woman in the newspaper on the bar counter beside him. He gazed at her arm cradling her massive breasts. Jesus, she had to hold those things up, they were so big. Almost like an arse. His fork was like a crane hire service, delivering chunks of ham and cheese sandwich. He started humming with pleasure. No particular song; something more like a speeded-up version of classical Western film music like *Big Country* or *A Few Dollars More*. He took a great draught of creamy black milk. He hummed and swallowed and chewed and looked sideways at the woman, as if he had something against her.

It was feeding time at the Haven. Jimmy pushed the trolley carrying trays along the corridor, the smell of tomato soup drifting before him. The nursing staff helped to distribute the trays to the various rooms: Mrs Broadbent, Mrs Bunyan, Dermot Banim, Bernard Berry, etc. Some of them were still able to handle their own lunch, more or less, though they sometimes dropped their spoons and had to call for help. Some made a big mess of themselves. Jam and butter all over their faces. Bernard Berry instantly slobbered soup all over his trousers.

84

Each tray had a bowl of soup, a knife, fork and spoon, a side plate with two slices of white bread cut diagonally across with a pat of butter. After he had delivered the trays, Sister Agnes asked him to take care of Mrs Broadbent who had already spent twenty minutes trying to open the butter. At this rate it would take her five days to finish the soup. Jimmy slipped the tip of the knife into the pat of butter, unfolded the edges and spread the soft yellow butter across the white triangles. Then he stuck the spoon into Mrs Broadbent's hand, a slice of bread in the other and stood back.

Off you go, Mrs Broadbent. I'm timing you.

Some of them wanted to go to the loo as soon as they saw the food. Others had to be spoon-fed. Nurse Boland normally spent a half an hour over soup with Mr O Reilly-Highland, pinning his head back against the armchair to stop him nodding. Even the triangular slice of white bread was a problem for some of them, because the tip flopped down and took them forever to aim at their mouths. Bernard Berry was trying to stick the bread in his ear.

Finally, when this daily drama was over and the Duphalac had been administered, Jimmy sat down in a wheelchair, looking out the window over the harbour, to eat a bowl of soup himself. He was hungry enough to be able to censor the grotesqueries of the old people's home out of his mind for the time being. Tried to convince himself he was not eating flaky skin and bedsores. Incontinence sheets. Mrs Spain's shrunken breasts. Polyps. Corns. Lesions and festering melanomas. Jimmy was beginning to feel jealous of the old people. And when Nurse Boland came into the sitting room, he started rattling his spoon against the side of the stainless steel bowl. Pretending to spill it all over the floor. Threatening to slobber and pee all over himself. Throwing slices of white bread around like paper aeroplanes until Nurse Boland smiled and knelt down in front of him to feed him with a mock frown.

Skipper Martin Davis had lunch on the move. He parked the red van on the pier and stepped out, took the wrapper off a tuna sandwich and opened a can of Sprite. The seagulls perched nearby and watched each movement of the food towards his mouth. He left the door of the van open so that the music on the stereo played to the open air.

It was a rushed meal, because Mongi had asked him to deliver a box of fresh fish.

Martin Davis threw the crust out on to the oily water where the gulls shrieked and fought for it. Then he walked over to the ice-box where the women sold a variety of fish. Two men from a Japanese restaurant nearby were picking and choosing. The skipper bought a full box of mackerel and the women were surprised that a fisherman would be buying fish. But Martin Davis side-stepped the enquiries by saying it was a special delivery to a catering firm.

Mongi O Doherty was a great man for the kiddie food. Beans, chips and sausages. He had not progressed to an adult diet yet, and his mother was cooking up some prime pork sausages for his lunch. She had crossed the city on a bus to get his favourite Hick sausages and now stood in the kitchen, staring out the window as she listened to the radio, all about a young boy who had been inducted into a religious sect and brainwashed. It would never have happened to her son, Richard.

Mongi was in the living room watching Sky news. Every now and again they would break in with the latest stock market reports and share index, which irritated him no end.

Does my head in, he said to himself.

For practical reasons, much of his money was tied up in property. He had recently bought the house and put it in his mother's name, though it was understood, of course, that an unwritten contract between mother and son was more binding than any legal document. His present address was at a city centre luxury flat where he spent most of his time with his present girlfriend, Sharon. Cooking was not one of her strong points, however, and Mongi usually ate at home with his mother.

Mind, the plate is hot, she warned, placing the meal of ebony sausages in front of her son. A life in waitressing had taught her how to distract from the food at a crucial moment.

What's this? Mongi demanded, looking at the disaster on the plate.

I was listening to this programme, she said. I got kind of carried away, son.

Don't call me son, Ma.

There was no excuse for incinerating a man's food. Unforgivable. It was worse than any double dealing. Worse than snitching. Worse than being fucked over by the law. His own natural mother, destroying the best of Dublin sausages as though she cooked them with a blowtorch.

They're black!

I'm sorry, Richard.

And look, Ma! Did I ask for parsley?

No, she said. I just thought it would look good.

What use was a touch of garnish when the rest was totally inedible?

It's pretentious, he said, picking up the lettuce and dangling it in the air. Especially when you go and burn the shaggin' sausages.

I'm doing my best, son.

You know what lettuce and tomatoes says to me. It's a set-up. A stake-out. It's just the kind of thing the cops would hide behind. I can see them hiding under that lettuce in plain clothes. Lettuce and tomato is a dirty Garda operation.

He picked up the knife and pointed it at his mother. Even if it was only a butter knife, it was enough to terrify her. Nobody had more power to scare a mother than her own son.

You're trying to shop me, Ma.

No, son. I'd never do that. I swear. My own flesh and blood.

Mongi ruthlessly pushed the greenery off the plate. His mother went back out to the kitchen and sulked, while he sat in the living room, trying to make the best of his meal alone. He took one of the ebony sausages and placed it on a slice of pre-buttered bread, drew a red line of ketchup along the top and rolled it up like a sleeping bag. He saw food basically as a victim. He bit the poor little sleeping sausage with a ferocious bite of his yellow smile, expecting it to scream in pain.

Mongi had subliminal thoughts about eating raw food. He looked at the Sky newscaster and imagined taking a big bite out of her arm. He wanted to return to the wholesale savagery of eating in the jungle, as though food didn't taste right unless he killed it himself. Perhaps he should have been a butcher.

He pushed the sausages away and turned to a bar of Toblerone. Something about the pyramid shape made it more of a challenge. He bit off a slice of the mountain, leaving the satisfaction of his teeth markings behind. Chewed and took a good sip of Southern Comfort. Churned the mixture around in his mouth, inhaled through the grid of his brown teeth and swallowed.

There was a knock on the door. It was the skipper, Martin Davis waiting outside with his box of mackerel.

Marlene Nolan opened a tub of Hot Cup, poured in the boiling water and watched the metamorphosis taking place in front of her eyes. It was a miracle each time, like the resurrection of Christ. The room lit up as the golden light radiated from the Hot Cup. The smell that permeated the flat was something close to a block-layer's armpit. She had got used to that reek and even began to crave it. Missed it when it was gone. It was like the bad smell they put into natural gas so that it could be detected by the human nostril, a scent that was designed to be thoroughly offensive but that you could get attached to, in a peculiar way. Maybe it reminded her of her father – his big overpowering, testosterone presence in a small two-roomed council house. Smiling with his white shirt rolled up at the sleeves, and the smell of stale smoke in his clothes mixed with his all-embracing Parmesan scent. A hundred thousand paternal armpits processed into one concentrated cup and brought alive with boiling water. She sat down and switched on the TV. A programme about dogs and dog owners. Taking care of your pet. How to vet the kennels.

Councillor Sylvester Hogan took a light lunch at the yacht club. He hadn't eaten there in a long time and was told the food had greatly improved. It had always been more of a drinking haunt, for meeting up with people from the Chamber of Commerce. They had changed some of the kitchen staff and had since received a Sense of Excellence award, as if excellence was some kind of absolute in itself. Excellent what?

Who knows. Perhaps the dining room was worth another go, Hogan thought.

The waiter greeted him with huge enthusiasm and behaved like a method actor as he ushered Hogan to a table, bowing and practically genuflecting; speaking in a broken French accent. But Hogan knew he came from Sallynoggin, just up the road, and had picked up the strange hybrid dialect as a commis chef in Paris.

Hogan could have told him that Irish people didn't like all this attention to be drawn to themselves when they were entering a restaurant. Eating out was still a stealthy engagement. And they didn't want it broadcast around the world on Euro News every time they had a snack in public.

The waiter stuck a menu into Hogan's face and stood back with gleaming pride.

Hogan went for the Seafood Symphony and bore an expression of supreme satisfaction when it arrived on the table. It was a dish in the great Irish tradition of pink prawn cocktails with orange mayonnaise sauce on a bed of lettuce and soft cherry tomatoes. A prizewinning College of Catering creation that came with slices of home-made brown sodabread which began to crumble in his hands as soon as he touched it.

Magnificent, he muttered as he opened the four provinces of the butter pat and tried to bind the breadcrumbs together.

Some day Hogan would start a gourmet charter for his country. Show people what a real gastronomic sense of excellence meant. He could talk. Some of the meals he had eaten on his fact-finding missions to Europe were absolutely stunning. Such class. Such aesthetic masterpieces. The German *Schweine-haxe* ranked among his favourites.

Hogan skipped the main course and moved straight on to the pudding. The new chef had concentrated on minimalism. A tiny piece of apple pie sat at the centre of a massive dinner plate. A piece of confection which came with a knife and fork and looked like a secluded thatched cottage on a deserted plain, with icing sugar and frosted snow covering the frozen landscape. Rural desertification, with boreens of chocolate designs all over the empty plate to signify a trend away from the land. A humble apple pie in a Southfork setting, with a dollop of cream like a marquis tent on the ranch.

Any other day, Hogan would have been a little disappointed with the portion. But that afternoon, he had set up an appointment with a healer. Carmel Coyne was going to meet him at his home to cure his back. He was smiling to himself as he demolished the apple cottage.

Corina Stanescu ate a plain hamburger and french fries. Initially, when she started working at a diner-style, take-away restaurant, she was excited about this kind of food, with its new world taste of prosperity. But she had by now watched at least a million customers devouring the same meal. It seemed to her that it was fantasy food; customers who came there were just mentally hungry and ate an imaginary meal. She had seen people impatiently cramming french fries into their mouths as if they could never get enough. There was something insubstantial about them, as though each person knew they were being cheated.

She remembered how in Bucharest people had taken the McDonald's trays home with them at first, thinking that everything was free, or else thinking that they deserved a little more. People had flocked with great excitement to the new fast food restaurants, as if they represented a new freedom. Her attitude had changed since she'd started working there herself. All she could think of now was the temperature of the deep frier, and the length of time it took to cook a hamburger, and the correct procedure with the garnish. At first, she hadn't noticed the distracted looks on customers' faces. Or the people who sat alone, not eating anything, just staring into the street outside and the passing traffic. Women with buggies. Men holding on to styrofoam cups.

The manager said Corina was very good at her job. He had told her that he was going to promote her permanently to the till. No more mopping up and collecting trays. No more frying burgers and preparing french fries. She was on the counter from now on, he said with a great big smile that must have meant something. He fancied her, that was for sure. He said she was very intelligent and that she had the ability to become a manager herself. But this only worried her even more.

As she finished her hasty meal, she understood at last what the hamburger and french fries were supposed to do. They triggered off subliminal memory of other food. Meals

back home in Romania, like *sarmale*, and *mititei*. And
papanasi.

Mr Killjoy was having his lunch at one of those wholefood
restaurants, run by a co-op of local women. Chicken in
white wine sauce, with rice and pineapple. Every dish on
the menu at the Whole Earth restaurant was his favourite.
Especially the desserts.

He took out the *Irish Times* and set it beside him on the
table. It was not a newspaper as such, but a device for
distracting attention from food. A utensil, needed for eating
your lunch; some kind of mental fork or psychological
shoehorn, on a par with any other cutlery. Killjoy needed a
decoy to make onlookers think that he was more interested
in the news than he was in food.

The presence of the newspaper allowed him to enjoy his
lunch without thinking that he was being watched. He
could eat heartily, uninhibited by the casual gaze of other
people. He could remain inside the closed circuit of his own
world, forking the chicken dish with one hand, pinning
down the paper with the other.

It was a platform of deceit. A form of food denial. As
usual in Ireland, everything operated on the reverse. If you
said one thing, then you meant something else altogether –
usually the opposite. Words and gestures were a bluster,
meant to convey what people wanted to hear.

It was only when Killjoy had finished his banoffee that he
could raise his head again and look around. Then he was
suddenly curious about what other people were eating,
looking at the mound of food the man next to him had on
his plate. And finally, when Killjoy sat back over his coffee,
he began to take on more global interests. He actually
started reading the paper.

Mongi was running his own catering operation, feeding fish
to the visitors out in Clondalkin. It was basically a piece of

monetary realism that helped to speed up what he called the wet-back repayments. Because he had failed to persuade Corina to enter into a more lucrative line of work, he would have to convince her in some other way. By leaning on her relatives.

Some of the Romanians were living in the low-density, car-dependent suburbs of Dublin, while Corina and a few other women lived in a flat in town. Her brother and cousin lived together in Clondalkin. Apart from some occasional shifts on building sites, they had found no permanent employment yet.

Mongi forced his way into a semi-detached house and found them sitting in the living room watching TV. Martin Davis put a box of mackerel down on the purple carpet. Looked around at the pattern of damp black stipple coming through the floral wallpaper in the corner. At first, it looked like he had brought them a gift. Some freshly caught fish. And though this turned out to be true, it was not quite what the Romanians had in mind.

Mongi was getting really pissed off, the skipper began to explain. He was there to give them a new deadline. He couldn't care less where they got the money. They could steal it if they liked. He wanted to be repaid in full by the following Friday.

Right, you fucking wet-backs, Mongi took over himself, making a call on his mobile. The amusements. It's time for some A -M-U-SAMENTS, he said, pronouncing the words as though they understood no English.

Caius and Tudor looked at each other.

Amusements, Mongi repeated. Amusamenteees. Amuse-mentescu or whatever the fuck you call it over there.

What are you doing? Martin Davis asked. He was beginning to feel nervous about this.

Mongi asked to speak to Corina Stanescu on the phone. There followed an altercation, along the lines that Corina was busy in the restaurant. So Mongi stressed the urgency of the situation. Said he was a surgeon at St Vincent's hospital. Talked about having to notify the next of kin, so the manager of the restaurant eventually capitulated and allowed her to come to the phone.

Corina Stanescu, Mongi said.

Yes, she said.

Mongi handed the phone to Caius. Then he took out one of the fresh mackerel – first of the season – and began to hold it up towards the young Tudor, brother of Corina. Caius talked quickly in Romanian, as if he was reporting on the scene.

Fresh fish, Mongi said. How do I know? Because it's stiff.

Rigor mortis, the skipper added, but he was not happy about the idea of fish being used as a threat. Fish were sacred.

Erect, Mongi pointed out, holding the freshly caught fish with its blue, green and black tiger stripes up to Tudor's face. Later on it will go limp again. That's how you can determine the time of death.

It was like a party line. Mongi indirectly communicating with Corina in the restaurant, through Caius and a thousand years of the Romanian language over the mobile phone. In turn, she was trying to deal with the restaurant manager who was getting angry behind her at the time she was spending on the phone. And he in turn was trying to deal with starving customers.

Mongi said no more. Just held Tudor's head back against the wall with one hand and pushed the fresh mackerel into his mouth, head first. Tudor struggled, but Mongi was in a dominant position for this force-feeding programme. Soon there was little more than the tail end sticking out. Like an unexploded torpedo.

This was all in the nature of a parable. Mongi was not seriously trying to feed fish to foreigners. It was merely a gesture, a liturgical offering which was relayed to Corina as an indication of what might happen if she didn't clear the debt by the given date. For the moment, Mongi was at pains to point out, this was strictly a symbolic feeding. The next time it would be real. And maybe not oral either. Then he took back the phone and spoke directly to Corina.

I'm giving you a week, Mongi said. Then they left.

Fred Metcalf was too old to eat lunch any more. He opened the box of Kentucky chicken and fed it to a range of cats who instantly arrived as though they could read his mind. He stood on the doorstep of his flat and threw them the chicken legs that Coyne had brought. In the background, the TV was on all the time, with the sound turned down. Silent figures of a daytime soap opera.

Fred's stomach had come to a standstill. All he ever ate these days was biscuits and tea. Mikado, custard creams, chocolate Kimberly. Anything that people brought to him at his small flat. But especially pink biscuits. Flamingo pink sponge. By now there was a large concrete block of pink, reinforced cement lodged in his abdomen. Surgeons said there was no point in operating. He was too far gone.

When the cats had been fed, he went back inside and sat down with a cup of tea. But even then he had no appetite. Instead he was transfixed by a commercial on TV. The agility of young people dancing and skating around in front of him was stunning. Here was the landscape of the future, full of young people leaping around and eating Pringles. Music punctuated by the amplified crunch of their mouths around the wafer-thin food. That's what youth was – hunger and energy and fun. Crunch! Crunch! Fred watched this high-speed meal with great awe. Once you start you can't stop. These people were eating themselves sick.

The take-away restaurant suddenly became packed with schoolboys in their crested college blazers. The windows were steamed up. You couldn't get in the door. They were all there for their usual burgers and hot dogs and french fries. But they were also there to look at the new woman behind the counter in her blue gingham overalls. Something about the way Corina looked each one of them in the eye as she served them. Something also about her foreign, East European accent drew these boys down from the nearby college every day. Some of them asked her irrelevant questions, trying to get her to smile. They laughed about hot dogs. Muttered in baritone voices as they ate. Threw straws of french fries at each other. Called each other wankers and gave each other wedgies, especially those preoccupied with the Romanian woman behind the counter with the smile and the shadows round her eyes.

The girls from Loreto Abbey were hanging around outside a local newsagents' shop. Mr Kirwin did a little pizza business every lunchtime and Jennifer and Nuala bought a slice each. Most of the older girls were having cigarettes: more tar, less calories. The convent girls were using as much bad language as possible, making up for lost time, when girls were sweet and full of Catholic ethos. Mr Kirwin seemed to put up with it most of the time. Will you fucking give us a fucking light you fucking bitch! Which was as sweet and polite as they were ever going to be to each other. I'll give you a kick in the clit, you cow! While Jennifer and Nuala ate their pizza, they watched as two older girls threw down their bags and challenged each other to a fight. There were no rules among girls any more. Biting, scratching and kicking were all legal. Knickers in the air to passing motorists. Skin and hair flying until Mr Kirwin, the United Nations shopkeeper, had to come out and separate them, saying Girls, Girls, Please! and offering Kleenex to the one with the bloody nose.

Mrs Gogarty had invited Carmel around for lunch to meet some of her friends. Nothing was spared in terms of effort and style. It was lunch in a formal sense. The full orchestra. The best delph. Silver cutlery, silver napkin rings and silver knife and fork rests so as not to stain the white tablecloth.

The main course was fresh grilled salmon steak with hollandaise sauce. New potatoes and fresh garden peas. All organically grown, as Mrs Gogarty was only too pleased to point out.

Carmel gave her some help in the kitchen, but everything had already been prepared. All Mrs Gogarty had to do was cut the fresh brown bread, and Carmel noticed how her mother leaned forward in a special bread-cutting posture, with the knife in one hand and the bread in the other. Everybody was equal in front of bread.

The women in Mrs Gogarty's circle had elevated the business of lunch to a showcase. It had less to do with food or the gratification of appetite than with the whole pageantry around the meal. For them it was more like a ritual. A stage drama which they revived and re-enacted every now and again to elevate food and remove it from the vulgarity of need.

Conversation ran along the lines of a daytime talk programme. Should drivers be allowed to use mobile phones while driving? By gum, one of the women said, they should not. Mind you, in defence of the mobile phone, another one of the guests said, it was great security to have one in the car. Finally, they moved on to horrific accidents. The fact that there was no crash barrier along the central reservation on the new motorway. The idea of a car coming across that central reservation straight into the oncoming traffic.

The idea behind this great lunch was to defy the existence of hunger and appetite. They had a way of eating salmon and hollandaise sauce without damaging their lipstick or leaving lip marks on wine glasses. It was more like a hunger test, to establish who could best conceal their appetite. Mrs Gogarty had learned all of this at boarding school down the country. Ladies ate bread before they went to a meal so they didn't end up behaving like a starving peasant. Never go to dinner hungry, Scarlett O'Hara's mother used to say. Because Irish people, no matter where they ended up, were taught to present a noble abstinence. It was food warfare. Mrs Gogarty ended the meal with a flourish, placing a basket of exotic fruit on the table with lychees and kiwis. The guests surrendered.

The poet with the four docile dogs was great on food phrases. He possessed a number of key lines in praise of food. Even though it was hospital food and he wanted to dig in as soon as the nurses brought the tray, he didn't feel right eating in public – in the public ward – without ritualizing the meal with a few of his phrases. Letting the other silent patients know how hungry he was. Fucking starving! The Irish had refined many lyrical disclaimers to allow the naked savage in his wine-coloured, leaf motif pyjamas to attack his food with as much right as anyone else and not feel guilty about it. I could eat a farmer's britches through a hedge. I could eat a camel's balls through the eye of a needle. I could eat a pregnant nun's arse through a chair.

Ms Clare Dunford was trying to keep her weight down. It would be a lifelong struggle. In the same way that people once struggled to keep fed, she now had to fight a daily battle to keep from being overfed. Life will always revolve around food and money, she thought. Whether you have it or not. That day she skipped breakfast, or more correctly, postponed it until lunchtime.

She decided to take in a sandwich at the hairdressers'. There was not enough time for the hair appointment, and lunch afterwards, before she rushed back to her patients. She opted to combine the two, and had already taken a bite out of a cumbersome chicken and salad submarine when she was asked to lean back to have her hair shampooed.

There was a momentary loss of reality as the hairdresser rubbed vigorously, almost forgetting that Ms Dunford was human. Just another disembodied head for shampooing, like pots were for scrubbing. Ms Dunford chewed and examined the ceiling. Cool rim of the basin on her neck, hot water on her scalp. She savoured the combined taste in her mouth, even as she obediently leaned forward again with a red towel over her head. Eventually, she got back to the sandwich and coffee while the hairdresser started clipping and talking.

It was a new experience, Ms Dunford thought. A little disconcerting too, to watch her reflection struggling with the submarine. She observed a menacing grimace on her face as she bit into the roll and the contents of chicken bits and tomato squirmed awkwardly out through the sides. Hand like a safety net underneath. Lower set of teeth coming forward, round cheeks rotating, a little frown on her forehead and her marsupial nose curling up as she sipped from the styrofoam coffee cup. She was appalled at the vision of her own animal desires.

By now, everything was covered with a layer of clipped hair. Under the gusting blow-drier, she thought about the concept of food. It was cerebral as much as physical. Phantasmal, even. Perhaps it would become a revolutionary new dieting technique, to look at yourself eating and to see at first hand the singleminded greed in your own eyes. Ms Dunford was so astonished by her eating habits that she pushed the submarine away. Only then did she notice that, with a touch of mousse, her head had begun to resemble a Donegal ram who had stopped grazing for a moment to look at a passing car: two great hanks of hair curling dangerously forward on either side of her face, and her lower jaw still swinging relentlessly.

Coyne took his time reading through the post-mortem report. There was nothing in it that pointed the finger at any murderer. Nothing that indicated foul play as such. Only the cause of death by drowning. The rope burn marks and an injury to the head which was assumed to have been caused by Tommy's head striking against the side of a boat during his fall. The report mentioned injuries consistent with motion.

Coyne was struck mostly by the details on Tommy Nolan's intestines. The pathologist had found considerable amounts of alcohol in his body. There was also evidence of chips, partially digested. Tommy must have gone up to the chipper before he went down to the harbour. That's why Coyne could not find him on the night in question. Because Tommy was standing in the Ritz waiting for a bag of chips. Probably looking at himself reflected in the convex stainless steel front-piece of the chipper. His face clownishly elongated as he waited.

Salt and vinegar?

On his way to the psychologist that afternoon, Coyne could not help thinking about Tommy's stomach. He imagined what everyone else had in their stomachs that afternoon. Like some laser vision, he could see into stomachs all over Ireland: a cross-section of the food that was consumed at lunch on a single day. Mikado biscuits. Sausages. Tomato soup. Chips. Fresh salmon. Chicken in white wine sauce. Chicken submarine. As though Coyne had carried out a national autopsy on the potato republic. Fresh garden peas. Beans. A slice of toast here and there. Biscuits with cheese. Cabbage and boiled potato. Hot dogs, doughnuts, sausages, Pringles and lychees.

Ms Dunford asked Coyne to sit in the usual chair while she started strolling up and down her office. She looked out through the window with her back to him.

Coyne appeared to have something to say that afternoon. He was unusually eager to talk, and lifted the embargo on his schooldays. Without realizing it, he was giving Ms Dunford what she was looking for.

I'll tell you about the bread and seagulls, he said.

It was in the school-yard. There were two gangs, with two dens. It was always like that, gangs running through the yard, clashing somewhere in the middle and retreating. The physical force tradition of the Irish school-yard. Coyne always kept his back to the wall and watched as they came. And then one day, in the middle of the yard, he saw one of them punch one of the younger boys full in the stomach. An innocent bystander.

He just doubled over, Coyne said. I turned around and saw him there with his mouth open, leaning forward. Holding his stomach with one hand. His sandwiches in the other. His mouth was wide open. But there was no noise. It was like a silent scream.

Coyne remembered a piece of masticated bread slipping from the boy's mouth. It hung on to his lip for a moment and then fell to the ground. And then all the other sandwiches wrapped in tinfoil also fell on the tarred surface of the yard while around them the warring continued. Boys with sticks and cardboard shields, shouting and flailing at each other in combat. The boy who was hit in the stomach, right in the middle of the war. Speechless. Screaming silently.

It was Tommy Nolan. Everybody was patting him on the back and asking was he OK. Are you all right? When the gangs retreated to their fortesses, Coyne picked up the sandwiches and put them back in the tinfoil wrapper. But Tommy's hands were limp and he dropped the sandwiches on the tarmac again.

He was winded, I suppose, Coyne said. That's why he couldn't make any noise. They called for his sister Marlene and she looked after him from there on.

The worst thing was afterwards, thinking about it. Coyne sitting in class looking out at the yard, all empty, with the echoes of the shouts still left behind. And the seagulls coming down to pick up whatever sandwiches were left lying around. They got Tommy Nolan's. They got every bit of crust and jam-tinted bread. They even got the half-masticated bit of dough that Tommy had in his mouth and let fall down with a dribble as he began to cry. Coyne was locked into these helpless endings. Condemned to repeat them in his head, unable to move on.

It was extraordinary, the amount of intimate details people were willing to give a healer. Because Carmel had the ability to take pain away, she was often entrusted with all kinds of personal matters. She commanded complete trust. Pain normally brought people to their knees. In the belief that she could take it away, they told her everything.

Carmel was, in the first instance, a good listener.

Because all else had failed, Councillor Sylvester Hogan was now relying on her to sort out the alarming state of his lower back. In his position on the borough council, he had been on junkets and visited healers all over Europe. No cure available.

Carmel sat in the living room of his house, with the bay window looking out at the stone lions on the gates and the harbour beyond. Hogan's wife Norma had gone for extensive beauty treatment. Leg wax, bikini line: she would be wrapped up like a mummy for the next four hours. A charity dinner engagement after that. Hogan asked Carmel to look on this session as open-ended.

I've tried everything, he said in despair. What I'm telling you now is monumental, he seemed to be indicating with his eyes flashing. Nothing was quite as destructive as back pain. He was close to tears.

It must be hard on you, Carmel encouraged.

It's hard on my wife too, he explained on an updraught of emotion. Heels sinking into the carpet of humility.

Carmel was swallowing hard. She was moved by his

honesty. In the silence, she heard a very audible stomach gurgle which could not be clearly attributed to either of them. They gave each other a look of denial. Hogan with libidinous recognition in his eyes.

Carmel told him to lie on his stomach, on the carpet of his own front room. In his Salvador Dali, melting-clock boxer shorts and with a pair of white porcelain greyhounds standing guard on each side of the fireplace, she began to examine his vertebrae, feeling each disk and then moving on, while Hogan pinpointed the pain.

Yeah, just there, he said. That's exactly the place. It's an atrocity.

She placed the big granite egg straight down on the base of his spine. Hogan was in ecstasy. Groaning into the carpet with relief. Submitting fully to the sorcery of stones. His energy flow was coming back slowly as Carmel counterbalanced the granite with other small basalt and limestone rocks and stones, until Hogan was covered in a pattern. Stoned to death in his own home. Call it accidental if you like, but Sylvie Hogan allowed his hand to make contact with her knee and take in the smooth sensation, like a soft, round, washed stone.

Late afternoon, Corina managed to appeal for compassionate leave. She went to the Anchor Bar to try and contact Pat Coyne.

I want to talk to Pat, she said.

Lot of people come in here by that name, the barman said. Besides, there was a matter of discretion here. A barman had to stick to the non-disclosure ethic of the confessional.

There was nobody else in the pub at the time except the poet, sitting in the snug with his crutches. He looked up at her and saw a vision of great beauty.

Raven black hair, he said. Sign of true Celtic blood.

Corina wrote out the name and number of a city restaurant on a beermat and handed it to the barman.

Who would he give this document to? The barman shrugged. She had to give him a bit of a description at least.

A goodlooking man, she said. With hair standing up on his head.

Lot of goodlooking fellas in here, the barman said.

Many a man in the Anchor Bar who'd do anything to receive a message from a woman like her, is what he wanted to say. She remembered that Coyne had told her something about being in a fire. So that narrowed down the handsome men of the Anchor Bar to a short list of one. The barman nodded and placed the beermat between two antique stout bottles behind the bar. Corina left.

The fact that she had mentioned a goodlooking man caused great derision around the bar. Throughout the afternoon and early evening, every crock of a man in a donkey jacket was sized up for the message like some male Cinderella. The whole pub was talking about Coyne's mystery woman.

Should have seen her, the barman kept saying. Fucking gorgeous, I swear.

What was her name? McCurtain wanted to know.

Corina, the barman answered.

The poet said she had to be a supermodel. Surrounded by all the men in the bar, he leaned on his crutches and drew an exquisite word-painting. A lyrical Identikit photo-fit picture of the young woman. And because McCurtain was such a good customer, the barman showed him the beermat.

It was a miracle. Sylvester Hogan got up from the stone therapy and walked. He was suddenly free from all pain. Carmel had liberated him from the greatest curse on earth and he wanted to jump around like a goat. Spring in the air and dance. He was a new man and put his arms around her with an exuberant embrace.

He was a man of property, he reminded her. But what use was all of this new wealth to him if he was a cripple who could hardly walk? At that moment in time, he was building a complex of fifteen Irish cottages on Achill Island. With the tax arrangements in place, they would effectively pay for themselves within five years. You couldn't help making money in this country: if you had any kind of intellect at all, the money was throwing itself at you.

Carmel sat on the sofa with Hogan. She had lifted the curse and saw the adoration in her patient's eyes. He wanted to repay her. Some reward fitting for this great miracle.

If you were interested in one of those holiday cottages, he said, I could see you right.

Ah now, Mr Hogan!

Sylvie, please.

Wait until you're absolutely sure the pain has disappeared, she said.

With a bit more regular treatment he would soon be in a position to go horse riding again. Golf at least. But you were never sure. Sometimes people went into remission. You didn't want to be making any rash promises and giving away Irish cottages. Carmel looked out at the lions on the gates. She wanted no reward, is what she was trying to explain. Her satisfaction came from the knowledge that she had done some good. She had brought the gift of health.

Thank the stones, she said.

You're a genius, he insisted. He was euphoric. Kissed her full on the mouth.

Jesus, Carmel! How could you have anything to do with a fraud merchant like Hogan? I mean, backache is the least of the things he should have. Somebody should go and break his back for him. Fold his vertebrae in two like a deckchair.

Snap! He deserves all the suffering he can get. He's a moral cripple with a derelict imagination. Did she not know that bastards like Hogan were responsible for all those trendy little Toblerone cottages, with high-pitched roofs and big PVC windows?

Those weekend love-shacks have nothing to do with Irish heritage. They're so fake, they wouldn't even put them on a John Hinde postcard. And that fucker never even goes to Achill on his holidays. So he doesn't care.

Have nothing to do with Hogan, Carmel. He's the town killer. He's the landscape killer. Give him back his low back pain. Make him suffer. Ram the stones up his arse. Snap his lollipop spine. Put him in a wheelchair and send him up to the Haven nursing home.

Again and again over the last year since they separated, Coyne had continued to act as Carmel's conscience. He tried to warn her and protect her from marauders and con men. But she was no longer listening. She had left behind the stone wall solidity of her relationship with Coyne. It was goodbye to poverty and peril. Goodbye to indigenous humility. Instead, she was entering into the spirit of new building materials. The security of arched doorways and Doric pillars. Fake stone façades and garden furniture. White balustrades and stone lions.

Carmel allowed Councillor Hogan to open some buttons on her dress. A summer outfit she had bought the previous day. She was at the forefront of a new healing age. Of PVC windows and draught-free doors. Of double garages and outdoor lighting. Underneath, she wore the new luminous green bra and knickers that Coyne had bought her. Eternity behind the knees and between her breasts. She was turning her back on the old Ireland. A consummate betrayal of the past. She was leaning against the wall in Hogan's living room, allowing him to lift her dress and remove her rebel green underwear.

Mind your back, she said, her breasts already spilling out of her dress.

Break his back, Carmel. For Godsake, cripple the bastard.

But Hogan couldn't care less about his back. Pain had a short memory and he was already laughing at it. Laughing at Ireland. Dancing on the graves of generations. Fecklessly snapping his spine in and out, like a great athlete. Man and superman! With his melted boxer shorts around his ankles and his buttocks flexing like the rump of a great stone goat god of mythology. One hand was propped against the wall for support. In the other, he held the luminous green knickers up to his nose and inhaled deeply.

Jimmy Coyne was out there spending money like a profligate son. He was with God and with Money. Every second day he was down at the foreign exchange desks in the various banks, looking up the rate of the American dollar. It was time he moved on to a new set of banks. These tellers were getting nosy. Soon they would be asking questions.

He was lavishing attention on Nurse Boland, taking her out to dinner in hideaway restaurants, buying her gifts – chocolates, drink, drugs, jewellery. Even got to the stage where Nurse Boland was beginning to ask where the money was coming from. The wages at the Haven were known to be the meanest in Dublin. The nuns had even deducted money for Jimmy's white overalls.

Most of Jimmy's expenses went not so much on material gifts as spiritual improvements. Occasionally, he was able to buy drugs from his friend Gussy. And Gussy accepted foreign currency, though he normally levied a stiff exchange fee. He also asked questions about where it came from and was promptly told to mind his own fucking business.

Jimmy declared himself to be independently wealthy.

He was only working to see Nurse Boland. In the boiler

room at the Haven he had hidden the holdall bag containing an endless flow of dollars. Happy ever after amounts of money.

Mongi O Doherty made a fortuitous breakthrough late in one afternoon. One of his dealer friends quite casually mentioned dollars. From time to time, Mongi used a bit of high-quality dandruff, but the coke circle was quite small. Initially he thought it was some kind of bad joke when the dealer asked him if he wanted to pay in dollars.

Are you fucking ragging me? Mongi said.

Jesus, no! I'm only saying, like, everybody else is paying in foreign money these days.

So there was a little spontaneous enquiry. And the trail very quickly led to the young Gus Mangan, a part-time dealer in coke, who was Jimmy Coyne's best friend. Mongi went around to visit Gussy, put a lighted cigarette up to his eye and asked him if he wanted to see the sun. Caught up with him in his granny's living room and showed him what the inferno looked like up close. Eventually came out with the name of Jimmy Coyne.

Jimmy was incredibly unlucky: the day he moved from virtual love into active love was the day that he got sacked from the old people's home. Most of the afternoon had been spent putting people in wheelchairs and bringing them outside where they sat overlooking the harbour with parasols overhead. Jimmy had done it all efficiently. It was not a problem with his work that finally caused his dismissal, but his desire for Nurse Boland.

He was caught in the act. The nuns were all outside with the old people. Only two or three of the residents had been left upstairs. Mr O Reilly-Highland, Mr Berry and a Mrs Cordawl who was so infirm she could not be brought down any more. Youth was a faraway country of the past.

In front of this audience of three distinguished guests,

Jimmy finally managed to win Nurse Boland over. He opened her uniform. She was a willing accomplice and assisted by removing her underwear. With the wheelchair audience gazing with open mouths at the sheer agility of their movements, Jimmy made love to Irene Boland for the first time. On a hot early summer afternoon.

Until big Sister Agnes dropped in.

Jimmy could not understand why Nurse Boland pulled away so suddenly. Was it some contraceptive instinct that made her jump and hide in the wardrobe? Leaving Jimmy with his trousers down, looking out over the harbour in a multi-dimensional dream.

What is going on? Sister Agnes shouted, as if there was an element of doubt. As if she was deceived by her own eyes.

Look, Sister Agnes, this is not what you think it is.

But the expression on Sister Agnes's face confirmed that she was not as stupid as she looked. She came from a farming background and knew very well what male buttocks were meant to look like.

I've seen all kinds of animals trying this kind of thing, she said, blessing herself.

She was built like a bodyguard. Should have been working as a bouncer in one of the night-clubs, the way she came over and lifted Jimmy up with one hand and dragged him half naked all the way along the corridor towards the sluice room. When Jimmy tried to resist, she threw a killer punch which almost knocked him out. As soon as he got dressed, he was dragged ignominiously out of the Haven on to the street. Lucky not to be taken away by the Gardai.

You beast! she shouted after him. Don't ever come near this place again. Ever!

Mongi O Doherty had a knack for being in the right place at the right time. He had been driven up and down through the coastal suburb all afternoon by an associate. He had passed by the Haven nursing home a number of occasions, but eventually caught up with Jimmy Coyne later on as he walked past Fitzgeralds' timber yard.

Jimmy had compensated for his bad luck by taking some afternoon narcotics. He was artificially elated as he wandered back home in the direction of the flat. Hardly noticed anything until it was too late. He was preoccupied with the fact that he had finally made it with Nurse Boland. He was in a dream. A big grin on his face, despite the almighty punch from God administered by Sister Agnes's fist, which was still throbbing in his jaw. Maybe his jaw was even fractured by the blow. It was a hoor to be in love, no doubt about it. But that was nothing in comparison to what was waiting for him.

Come 'ere, you fucking dirtbird bastard.

Mongi got out of his car and crossed Jimmy's path, carrying a wheelbrace. His assistant came around the other side of the car to make sure Jimmy had no escape. Gus Mangan, Jimmy's best friend, stayed in the back of Mongi's car, with his head down.

Jimmy was at the height of his powers of alacrity and cunning, however. The drugs and sex should have induced a benign acceptance of the world, but they also elevated his self-preservation instinct. He realized that his genes faced rapid extinction. Something about the look on Mongi's face told him that he was facing a straight Darwinian contest for survival. It was like any ordinary Sunday afternoon wildlife programme, with Jimmy as the zebra cutlets, Mongi as the greater shovel-nosed debt collector. Capitalism equalled chaos, was the basic message to be extracted here. It was the natural order of things, and Jimmy owed this man money, simple as that.

It is behoving on you to give yourself up, Mongi demanded. Surrender, you little fucker.

Instead, Jimmy made an instinctive detour. His legs were programmed to make a run for it, rather than attempting any kind of serious dialogue. This was not the time for conflict resolution. He ran towards the timber-yard gates, which were closed. Managed to get a foothold on a low wall and heave himself up. Mongi and his mate were close behind. As Jimmy tried to get across the gate, puncturing his hand and thigh on the barbed wire along the top, Mongi took the wheel brace and repeatedly jumped up, trying to hit Jimmy's head.

Always go for the head, Mongi explained, as though he was reading an extract from a Marxist manual. Everything feeds the capita. Always take the principal sum.

But instead of hitting Jimmy's head and eliminating any chance of escape, Mongi only managed to hit his arm and his elbow. Just as his prey was beginning to get away across the gate to safety, Mongi hit Jimmy another prizewinning blow on the ankle. The wheel brace sought out that perfectly rounded, cupboard knob of the ankle bone with such a clean strike that it made a note, like the sound of a tuning fork, resonating with pain as Jimmy fell down on the far side. He couldn't walk. He was hopping around on one foot, trying to contain the screaming musicality of this long note in his ankle. Humming and holding a high C across the whole city like a howling lament.

Mongi and his partner climbed up on to the wall. They both wore tracksuits which made them look very athletic.

Jimmy's problems were only beginning. He tried to limp away from the pain towards a stack of timber. Smelt the wood and creosote all around him. Noticed the gleaming blade of the power saw reflected by the yellow light from the street. Imagined the pain of his ankle being sheared away like a piece of turned mahogany and his foot dropping down on to the pile of sawdust like a cheap offcut. The sawdust going pink with blood. The psychedelia of fear.

At that moment he understood the full implications of survival. Why tabloid newspapers were always raising public consciousness of pain and pleasure, increasing the threshold of feeling. Why everybody had become so obsessed with violence and gratification. He longed to be back in the arms of Nurse Boland. Felt the warmth of her body luring him into submission.

In his intoxicated state Jimmy saw the rotary blade of a power saw running towards him out of the semi-darkness. He knew it was a common Alsatian guard dog, but he perceived it as an electric saw, spinning and whining as it came bounding through the timber aisles on four legs. Tungsten-tipped teeth and a long, purple-pink tongue dangling. Jimmy took another final leap of gene loyalty on to a stack of cut-price batons. The law of the jungle. Where an enemy can suddenly become a protector. When the sum of what you owe to one predator is equal to what that predator owes another.

You're dead, Mongi shouted as he threw the wheel brace at him. But it missed the target this time and clattered ineffectually along a shelf of planks. Jimmy was safe for the moment, protected by the dog barking continuously like a vicious peacekeeper. There was nothing they could do but watch Jimmy making his way to the other side of the timber yard, climbing from one island of wood to the next until he escaped across the far wall and limped off down a laneway.

Coyne responded quickly to the distress call from Corina. It was exactly what his life needed: a rescue operation, a humanitarian mission. He went to the take-away restaurant and found her wearing a paper hat and a uniform. Held up the queue of hungry customers, told them to have a bit of patience while he asked her some questions. She was reticent and embarrassed: kept looking around at the manager, who was staring at her with a smile that was like a slug curling up in salt. Corina kept telling Coyne to order something. This was no place to start explaining what had happened.

Is there some problem here? the manager eventually

asked, and Coyne ordered a strawberry-flavoured milk-shake.

He said he would wait till she finished work, and sat there like one of the lonely men staring into the distance all evening as if struck by some evangelical vision. In the old days they would have hung around in churches. Coyne watched the customers coming and going. The same routine repeated into infinity over a thousand times. People entering with expressions of hope and joy, staring in awe at the board where the menu was written up, then sitting down in the purple chairs, urgently hand-feeding themselves and leaving again in a bewildered state of grace.

Every now and again a young man came around with a brush or a mop to clean the floor or to clear away the trays. Outside the light was fading and giving way to night, while inside the restaurant was bleached in a bright fluorescent wash that showed up every blob and blemish.

They attacked my brother, she said, when Coyne finally escorted her away from the place. She outlined her predicament. The threats made against her if she didn't pay up.

She and twenty-four other people had paid their passage by boat, and now had to pay a second time because the money had been stolen. She had been forced to collect a levy from each of them and pay over the ransom in weekly instalments. Now the men were demanding the whole lot, within a week.

Don't let them give you a hard time, Coyne insisted. I'll deal with them. I'll sort out those bastards.

She smiled. It was a brave thing to say; gallantry from another epoch. He was ready to lay down his life for her and take on the agents of exploitation. He did not tell her that he was an ex-Garda, because he didn't see himself as a Garda any longer. And the Gardai were the last people to deal with this. As always, he had a plan.

You've got to get out of that place, Coyne said. You can do better than that.

It's a start, she said.

Your luck is going to change, he promised.

I don't know, she said.

She invited him inside her flat. He didn't want to intrude, or appear as though he was looking for a reward, but she begged him not to refuse her hospitality. Insisted on offering him a drink in the kitchen. Corina's brother and cousin were there. They repeated the story of their assault, detail by detail, and Coyne listened to every word with great anger. Vowed to kill the men who had carried out this attack.

Wait till they deal with me, Coyne said with an earnest expression, hair standing up on his head as if to prove he meant business. They made a big miscalculation, the bastards. Don't worry about it. It's all sorted out.

The women in the flat came and shook hands with Coyne. He had difficulty pronouncing their names, but he gave it a try. Smiling at them all.

It was like the old days in Ireland, when a visitor changed everything. The visitor brought the excuse to abandon life and step into a temporary fantasy. It was like walking into a house in Beal an Daingin when Coyne was a boy. Everything stopped. These people knew what the real welcome meant. They understood the feckless impulse of hospitality that was needed to make this the last great occasion on earth. They knew how to stop time; how to create a life-affirming moment of immortality. To laugh in the face of tragedy.

Coyne might well have stepped into their homes in Romania. They ushered him to a small table and made him sit down. Cleared the cups and food away and placed an unmarked Napoleon bottle of home-distilled plum brandy down. Filled tumbler glasses to the brim and stood back, talking all the time and watching him with pride.

Tuica, Corina said. Go on, drink up.

Coyne sipped the firewater. It was like *poitín*. Rocket fuel that went straight to his head. Jesus, they should mark that bottle with a skull and crossbones, he thought. He would be drunk for a week on this. Then start seeing white flashes. But he was ready to give everything to this spontaneous celebration. Nothing but complete abandon.

They offered him cigarettes even though he didn't smoke. Opened a new packet in front of him. Big white Smirnov ashtray. Romania was the last great refuge of smokers, they said.

Corina took on the role of interpreter. She described the journey to Ireland by trawler. Stuck in the cabins all the time, with no light and the smell of fish and diesel fumes in the air. Some of them vomiting because they had never been at sea before, not even on the Black Sea. Tudor recalled the fish diet he had been given. They were almost apologetic about it and kept saying how friendly the Irish were in general. OK, people kept mentioning Dracula, but that was easy to handle. It was the Irish who had invented Dracula in the first place.

Coyne raised his glass to them all. He was already spinning with passion. Toxic with emotion and charting the great undiscovered link between Ireland and Romania.

Of course, he thought, it was the sad gene. Here they were at last, the emigrants returning to Ireland. The Blasket Islanders. The famine people coming back in their coffin ships. *A stór mo chroí, when you're far away from the land you will soon be leaving.*

It was true, you could never escape history. For Coyne, however, the past was far more real, far more genuine than the present; his imagination far more vivid than reality. He could only see those parts of Ireland that had already disappeared. The great paradox of emergence and loss. He should have taken more notice before it was gone, during the glorious pre-television peak of Irish civilization. The past was like a lost lover. He should have known that this was the end of Ireland. Now it had leaped ahead into a new age of golf courses and windsurfing. Golf was the heart of Irish culture – that's what they were saying in the ads.

Coyne was trying to reverse time. Desperately clutching on to history in the same way that he was clutching at the lapels of Carmel – begging her to go back to the old days when love was simple. But she was having none of it. Coyne doggedly held on with that undignified and cloying embrace that eventually drives loved ones further away.

He was requesting the impossible. Trying to preserve everything like a museum. Begging the people of Ireland to wear the old clothes. The red dress and the lace-up boots. The Galway shawl. Pampootees! He was pleading with them to go back to currachs and Connemara hookers. Turf smoke and damp cottages. Put the rags up against the back door to keep the rain out. Hang the spiral fly trap from the light in the middle of the room. Carmel had become inaccessible. A figure of nostalgia, drifting away out of reach into the history books. Into black and white, Father Browne type photographic collections. Soon he would no longer recognize her, just as he could no longer recognize the Irish landscape.

Coyne was whirling with the effects of plum brandy. And still the Romanians were filling up his glass and pressing cigarettes on him which he couldn't smoke. He stood up with his glass to make a statement.

Welcome to Ireland, he said.

They stood up with him, and held their glasses up. To Ireland, they said.

It's not much of a country, but you're welcome as the flowers in May to any part of it. As long as you don't start playing golf. That's the only thing I'd like you to do for me.

Don't take up golf, for Jaysus sake. This country is blighted by golf courses already.

They thanked him, then swiftly moved into the dancing phase before Coyne got a chance to start talking again. It was only nine o'clock in the evening and Corina was urging Coyne away from the table into the middle of the kitchen.

You ain't nothing but a hound dog . . .

Corina led the way. In her loose, flowery red dress, she was showing Coyne how to relax and step outside himself. My God, these Romanians had something to show the Irish. They understood dancing the way it was meant to be. No more of the pseudo-Irish dancing with the wiggle of the hip. This was rock 'n' roll with gypsy blood. All they had to do was raise their arms, click their fingers, clap their hands and the whole room was dancing. One shoulder held provocatively forward and a look of powerful defiance in their eyes. There was no stopping them. Corina and Coyne jiving around at high speed with Caius and Tudor and some of the other women dancing in the background until the floor of the little kitchen was throbbing like a trampoline. The window shook in time to the music. As though rock 'n' roll had just been invented.

Coyne danced like a madman. A truly international epileptic explosion of boogie, shuffling, jiving and set dancing. Even if his head was incapable of commanding his limbs and the control of his legs was lost in a juddering mêlée, it was clear that he was having fun. He was enjoying this night in spite of himself. Having a ball for once without a single Irish person in sight. Perhaps his audience had finally disappeared. That night, Coyne appeared to lose all the inhibitions laid on his shoulders. He was abroad. Away from Ireland in a strange land of dancing and swirling plum brandy.

Later when they were exhausted he sat down with Corina alone. They talked for a while about Bucharest. About going for walks in the park every Sunday with her parents.

There would be peony roses out now. She was homesick at times. And Coyne once again found himself in a fatherly role, as though he had adopted her as a daughter.

The familiar streets of the borough were like an anticlimax. He was back in Ireland, walking home along the usual route with the sound of his own footsteps. Gateway after gateway, he passed by the gardens with their ornamental stones. All over the place, people were bringing more and more stones up from the shore. Every night Coyne noticed the latest additions. New oval-shaped boulders outside hall doors. Silly little lawn borders. Stone circles around rose beds. It was a great abuse of the natural world, forcing these rocks into suburban slavery. Coyne was ready to pick up one of their designer rocks and throw it through a front window. One night he would come down with a wheelbarrow and collect all of these stones and bring them back to the sea.

It seemed that the brief euphoria of dancing with the Romanians would inevitably be followed by some trauma. Even before he turned the corner into Cross-eyed Park and in through the garden gate to his own flat, there was a premonition of disorder. His flat had been ransacked. As he climbed the stairs, he saw the door ajar and the bootprint close to the lock.

Fuck, he uttered. His flat looked like a handbag turned inside out. Clothes everywhere. Documents scattered. Cupboards emptied out.

Coyne felt the calmness evaporate. He was suddenly exposed again, not only to the audience in his head, but to his enemies. The place no longer belonged to him. It was draughty and public, as though the doors could never be shut again and the intruders had taken away all sense of privacy. His flat was basically open to the street now. What worried him more was that nothing was taken. Just stuff thrown around the place as if they'd been looking for something specific. It was almost like a police search.

A box of photographs lay scattered across the bedroom floor. This is what he had taken away with him from the marriage: a tin biscuit box full of images. Not once since he had moved out had he opened that box, because he saw it as a last resort. Photographs of the children when they were small. Of Carmel and Coyne together laughing. Of Nuala and Jennifer on the swing. And lots of photographs of Carmel and the children from behind, looking out over the sea – the ones that Carmel always put away because she said they were depressing. Now they all lay on the floor. He knelt down and began to pick them up, looking at each one of them carefully before putting it back in the box.

It was the symbolic force of the intrusion that burdened him. The thieves had stolen something intangible. Something that could not even be identified in words.

Coyne attempted to put a few things back in place. Lifted a chair, closed a cupboard door. He thought of reporting it to the Gardai and knew he should leave everything the way it was. He wandered around looking at the mess of his own home. Going from one room to the other saying fuck! Tried to convince himself that it was a normal break-in. He had dealt with a lot of this, as a Garda. But he was increasingly aware of the fact that this was a search, not a robbery. He went through a subconscious inventory of belongings. Maybe that invisible item would be found missing months later. All items of commercial value were untouched. TV. Video. Ghettoblaster. What else was there to break into Coyne's flat for. The toaster? Bath towels that Carmel had given him last Christmas?

Where was Jimmy? Coyne phoned home and talked to Nuala. Carmel was out and Jimmy was taking a bath. Coyne knew that his son had something to do with it. What kind of stuff had he got himself involved in? He suspected drugs. He had seen the result of these hasty searches, normally accompanied with a dead body. He was unable to close the door of the flat because the wood around the lock was split.

He walked briskly to his former home. It wasn't far away, but the landscape began to unnerve him. When he turned the corner into the familiar street, he was assailed by the memory of his old life. The fact that he had left home had less to do with Carmel than with the oppression of this neighbourhood. It's these bastards he was getting away from, with all their own suburban ideologies. Mr Gillespie, the nocturnal golfer next door. And Mrs Brindsley across the road, with her B&B and dog minding service. At night, the tourists checked in and in the morning packs of dogs emerged with grotesque regularity. Dogs barking at the gates of hell every time you passed by the garden. Mrs Brindsley with her authentic seashore pebble driveway and her DIY identity.

There was a car parked outside his home. A Mercedes.

He stood back. Took cover behind a hedge that hung over the garden wall on to the pavement. He could see Hogan and Carmel in the car together. Leaning towards each other. Talking and kissing.

Coyne reached a depth of depression. There was nothing he could do, in spite of the fact that his methodology had always been characterized by instant action. Insurrection! A call to arms! Everything in Coyne's life had to be solved by generous deeds, often involving great personal sacrifice. He wanted to go and rescue Carmel from this bastard. He was ready to make his move, ready to drag Hogan out and impale him on the Mercedes emblem of the bonnet. He'd break his fucking back for him. Jesus, Hogan would be in a wheelchair, pissing himself.

The problem was that Carmel did not want to be rescued any more. She had been seduced by the new Ireland. And if Coyne resorted to force, he would end up driving her into Hogan's arms. Coyne was helpless, hiding on his own street. Standing in semi-darkness behind a hedge with a shadow turning his face half black half white, and with strands of spider silk drifting across his head around his ears and neck. He looked like he was waving at Mrs Brindsley's bedroom window for a moment. A frantic signalling in the dark, struggling with a web, thrashing his arms around to free himself from these fine strings.

He saw Carmel stepping out of the car with a bag of stones in her hand. She leaned back in for a moment before stepping away and laughing across her shoulder. Waving goodbye without looking back at the Mercedes as it pulled away.

Jimmy had been immersing his ankle in hot water, but it was not doing him much good. He was still limping when he emerged from the bathroom an hour later. His ankle had turned dark purple. He got some of his clothes together. He would go on the run. The flat in Cross-eyed Park was no longer safe. Nurse Boland was the only person who could provide a safe house away from the attentions of Mongi O Doherty. Away from the attention of his own father.

He had left it too late.

Coyne was at the door already, ringing the familiar bell. Nothing had changed here except that Coyne was now an outsider. A stranger.

Is Jimmy there? he asked when Carmel opened the door. He was so disturbed that he could not bring himself to be civilized and say hello.

Carmel laughed. She was nervous. Had Coyne been following her? She had just had time to take off her coat when Coyne had pounced on the doorbell.

Pat! Look, it's past midnight.

Coyne looked desperate, standing on the doorstep with the porchlight casting a melancholy shadow around his eyes. A hurt man. He had forgotten to shave and looked stubbly. Out of touch with civilization. Like he needed somebody to bring him back to earth and tell him when to change his shirt and brush his teeth. Carmel's heart went out to him. That orphaned boy-at-the-window look. But she could not invite him in. Not now. He would make her feel guilty. Kill all her privacy.

Come back in the morning, Pat. Let's talk tomorrow.

Coyne snapped out of his trance when he saw the bag of stones at the foot of the stairs behind her. Can I borrow your keys? he asked.

In the moral confusion, Carmel didn't know what to say. It was a spontaneous payment. She was buying silence. The fact that she put up no argument, and didn't even ask why he needed the car, said it all. An admission of guilt.

I need it in the morning, she said, dropping the keys into his hand. Not allowing his hand to touch hers. Not allowing his eyes to look into hers.

Jimmy came down the stairs and Coyne told him to get into the car.

Where are you going? she asked at last, but there was no explanation.

We're going to sort this out, he said.

He drove away as though they were never coming back. With an alarming yelp of tyres, he turned out into the street. Jimmy was afraid, not knowing what his father had in mind. He was almost craving the quantifiable threat of Mongi O Doherty. At least that was simply a matter of money, whereas Coyne remained utterly silent, locked into a kind of ideological riddle with no answer.

Coyne drove like a maniac. There was no other way to drive the small red car that Mrs Gogarty had bought Carmel. Past the Garda station. Screeching around the corner on to the main street. Feckless and furious. Turning towards the harbour and down to the very spot where Tommy Nolan had met his death.

Not here, Jimmy pleaded, looking around and expecting to see Mongi lurching towards him with the musical wheel brace.

Why not? Coyne said suspiciously. Was the truth coming out at last?

He stopped the car and left the engine running. The moment of reckoning.

They were parked near the edge of the quay. Nothing between them and the harbour now, not even a rope or a bollard. Just a step away from the surface of the black water. In the distance, some moored yachts swinging from side to side. Trawlers elbowing each other as they rose and fell on the tide. Nobody around: not a soul to witness this impromptu courtroom in a car. Just the cheap whine of the engine and the utter silence between them.

Did you do it? Coyne asked with great solemnity.

What, Dad?

Coyne revved up the car. The engine hummed.

Tommy Nolan? I want the truth. Why have they ransacked the flat?

I don't know, Dad. I didn't go near Tommy.

The truth, Jimmy, that's all.

Coyne let the handbrake down. Edged the car forward as if he had already made up his mind. Collective suicide. The most honourable way for them both to go. The truth involved sacrifice and he was ready to go with his son.

Jimmy began to cry. He was still only a boy, for Godsake. What could he say? He was dealing with Coyne's justice. A kind of double-bind test. The self-implicating verity fork. Because no answer could reach the absolute standard of truth set by his father. If he denied the murder of Tommy Nolan once more they would both be in the harbour, struggling with the fuel-laden gunge coming into the car.

The headlights of another car flashed over the water in front of them. It was like a door opening, letting in a shaft of light across the boats. Perhaps it was Mongi O Doherty coming to rescue Jimmy from his own father, inching slowly past the shipyards, down to the quays. Casting huge moving shadows, a candle coming down the stairs. Past the barracks. Right down to the foot of the pier where it stopped and the headlights went out, as if the door had closed again.

Coyne looked straight ahead. His breath was noisy, making a big sawing noise, keeping time with the crisis.

Jimmy looked around at the yellow half-darkness where the other car was now parked. Yellow eyes watching. Jesus, if it was Mongi, then he might as well die, here and now, with his father.

Go ahead, Jimmy said at last. Go ahead and drive.

Coyne turned to his son. He was clearly surprised and elated by this response and looked right into Jimmy's eyes as though he had witnessed a great redemption. He pulled the handbrake up and switched off the engine. Tears in his eyes. Tears in Jimmy's eyes too, knowing that he had given the correct answer by sheer accident. Jimmy had shown himself to be made of the same noble stock as his father. He was ready to die to uphold the truth.

By Jesus, Jimmy!

Coyne got out of the car, went round to Jimmy's side and opened the door. Nodded to his son to step out, then embraced him with a vice-grip hug. Jimmy's ribs were nearly crushed right into his spine. His shaggin' vertebrae were coming out through his mouth and his lungs punctured with the weight of paternal affection. Coyne kissed his son vigorously on the cheek to complete this extraordinary ritual. The trial on the pier.

I knew you didn't do it, Coyne said in triumph. I knew all along.

Then he let go of his son and they both stood for a while looking into the solemn black water below. They had just dumped some great secret into the harbour and were watching it long after it disappeared. They understood each other fully – they had entered into a great lie together.

You're my son, Coyne said with great feeling. I'll protect you.

Thanks, Dad!

Jimmy wiped his eyes with the back of his hand, trying to look like a man, and nervously glancing up the quay.

In perpetuity, son. I'll protect you in perpetuity.

Coyne slapped him on the back, a reward for his bravery. Of course, there were other questions that needed to be asked, but the communion of minds put matters of a practical nature on hold. It was a genuine father and son, funicular type relationship – pulling each other, but in opposite directions. An equal and opposite interdependence. Coyne didn't want to know anything else, because that bright blue kernel of understanding had been located. They didn't need to say a word more. They had postponed the truth. A dizzy reprieve, with the smell of fishboxes and engine oil all around them.

There was somebody whistling. It echoed across the water towards them and Coyne turned to see a figure approaching with a torch, beaming along the quay. Jimmy thought of making a run for it, but Coyne pushed him back into the car and got ready to drive away again.

It was Sergeant Corrigan. Whistler of all people had to come down and catch father and son staring into the harbour. This didn't look good at all, Coyne realized. Whistler, the plain-clothed Holy Ghost standing on the pier with his torch shining from below, making a mental note of the circumstances.

Coyne rolled down the window and smiled at the sergeant, as much as to say: What the fuck do *you* want?

Are you looking for Jesus or something? Coyne said as he drove away.

Sergeant Corrigan staggered backwards, a strange epiphany glowing across his face. A grin of sanctity. An apostle in plain clothes, standing on the pier with the beam of his torch entering his open mouth and lighting him up like a luminous souvenir.

Were you really going to go in? Jimmy asked on the way home again.

No way, Coyne said.

You were only bluffing?

Christ, Jimmy. Do you think I was going to kill us both?

It was a strange denial which increased the terror in retrospect. In the awkward silence that followed, Jimmy began to experience the full aftermath of fear, when the moment of crisis had passed and the clarity of this bizarre Russian roulette sank in.

They had started building a wall on the street where Coyne lived. As he came out of the flat the next morning, he saw that a truck full of granite rocks had been delivered and men were out there already with their cement, laying the foundations. A piece of twine had been spanned from a gatepost to the far end of the front garden and one of the men was placing the first of the granite rocks into an open trench.

Coyne watched them for a moment with fascination. The same way that he had watched men building dry stone walls in the west as a boy. Here at last was a job Coyne would like to have done himself. He could ditch his career and become a wall builder like these men. He admired the simplicity of the job, the plain sense of achievement.

One of the men wore a woollen hat on the side of his head like Toulouse-Lautrec. Coyne watched him slap cement on to the surface, then cautiously select a granite rock and place it on the cement. He tapped it into place with the handle of the trowel before stepping back to examine the progress from a distance.

This was a real job, Coyne thought.

Coyne went to visit Fred Metcalf, bringing another box of chicken nuggets with him, and some Kimberley biscuits. There was a time when he used to tell Fred everything that went on in his life. But now he had become a little more guarded and they talked merely in an agreed tone of melancholia.

Fred was going through a bad time. He was on multiple medication and had finally received a hopeless prognosis from his doctor. The obstacle lodged in his intestines was immovable. Fred Metcalf, the security guard, was going to die like Elvis, with a cement block in his stomach.

Coyne put on the kettle and they sat for a while and talked, because that was all that was left to do. Fred didn't even eat biscuits any more. Packets of them were piling up on the kitchen cupboard. He was wasting away.

They're not being honest with you, Coyne said. Doctors are liars.

Nothing they can do now, Fred whispered.

I'd put them under pressure. Demand the best consultants. I'm sure there's something they're not telling you.

But that was far too much hope for one afternoon. There is nothing more irritating to a terminal patient than the sound of blind optimism. Fred had no time for hospital waiting rooms. He was basically like Coyne. He didn't want to be cured. What was the point?

Diabolical, was how Fred put it. He was not just talking about his own health but the health of the nation.

It's not fair, Coyne said.

Look at them all dancing around, eating Pringles, Fred said. Everyone smiling at each other all the time. You'd think they had some disease or other that was making them soft in the head. Happy as pigs in shite all of them.

I know what you're saying, Coyne agreed.

Everything is great, Fred said. Everything is cool and wonderful. Everything is a masterpiece. A *tour de force*. A triumph. The whole country is praising itself out of existence. All these empty superlatives. One of these days they're going to run out of superlatives, Pat.

Absolutely, Coyne colluded. There's nothing ordinary.

Fred and Coyne had long been of one mind about the decline of civilization. They were staring up the same areshole of gloom, so to speak. Two men with grave expressions on their faces, belonging to the elite club of global paranoia, with only a minimum of sunlight entering the room through the small window, and the certainty of Fred's slow but imminent death underpinning the decline. Both of them brought up on tragedy, war and doom expectancy which they were forced to remained loyal to. An ancestral readiness for disaster. As if they were waiting for the return of the bad days and deeply mistrusted the new optimism and fun: the forces of darkness and remembrance fighting a constant battle with the forces of brightness and forgetting. One of these days that optimism would fall flat on its face. Then Coyne and Fred would have the last laugh.

Yeah, but are they happy? Fred asked triumphantly.

Good question.

You can see right through all this aerosol happiness. It's fake.

They're only putting it on, Coyne said. Maybe Fred was right. Maybe the Irish were basically a sad people who pretended they were happy, just waiting for the next calamity. Going to all kinds of clownish extremes to deny their melancholia.

It's the dogs of illusion, Fred concluded, shaking his head.

In the afternoon Coyne almost ran into his bank manager again. This time he was standing outside the book shop in the shopping centre. The town-killing Dun Laoghaire shopping centre. The ubiquitous Killjoy was now beginning to follow Coyne around, it seemed. Coming to haunt him after all the telephone calls. Maybe the Bank of Ireland had a long memory and had started cloning dozens of Killjoys, distributing them throughout the borough to stalk Coyne.

Mr Killmurphy was staring straight at him. Giving him the evil eye. Ready for confrontation.

It reminded Coyne to make more phone calls and to be more consistent in his campaign. Killjoy looked a little too happy. In fact, it appeared that Killjoy was saying something to Coyne across the distance. Killjoy looked like he was going to come over to talk to him.

In the background, George Michael was screaming *Freedom!*

Coyne had to make a swift detour to try and avoid Mr Killmurphy who was now coming towards him with a big grin on his face. Even had his hand up to indicate that he wanted to engage Coyne in conversation. To accuse him. Or maybe to ask for a truce.

Fuck off, Killjoy. You can't talk to me.

As Coyne made his escape along the rail, sprinting almost, with a shopping bag dangling beside him, he could see in the corner of his eye that Killjoy was diligently giving chase. It was like one of those Olympic walking races, where the contestants are not allowed to run. Killjoy galloping along with lots of torso movements and elbow power.

Coyne managed to get to the elevators, but then discovered that both were going up. It was typical of the town-killing shopping centre management to trap people on the upper floor to prevent egress. The twin elevators of no return. The inward and upward valve of shopping mall psychology.

Coyne, almost caught, got away just in time. He had to act fast, and eventually escaped by running down the hallway towards the next exit. Killjoy calling after him: Hello! Excuse me!

By afternoon, the wall outside Coyne's flat was almost finished. He stopped to admire the work. The men had gone home and a temporary barrier had been erected around the site. Coyne stood for a while examining the pointing and the skill with which the builder had selected his rocks. The cement was still drying, but the wall was already indestructible.

It was a masterpiece, of course, but he didn't want to start breaking into superlatives, going over the top and saying it was a brilliant wall. Or that no wall had ever been built like it. It was such an original wall. A new wall. A *tour de force* wall.

For Christsake, no. A wall was a wall.

He admired it quietly for a moment and went inside. The different shades of granite merging into a pattern. It was a fine wall.

At the harbour bar, McCurtain was drunk and acting up. He was annoying two local lads who had come back home on a visit with their German wives. They had just returned from Munich for the first time, visiting relatives, spending money and buying pints for all their local friends and neighbours. But McCurtain was full of drink already and took exception to them. He felt that these two feral homing pigeons didn't look quite right. They were too tanned and well dressed, taking their affluence to extremes, laughing and joking with the locals in a thick Dublin accent laced with a Bavarian swagger. The language of lederhosen made McCurtain bitter. It was sheer jealousy. One of the women was wearing glossy lipstick, and the pink print of her lips was embossed on the rim of a pint glass.

Where are you from? McCurtain asked.

Munich, one of the women answered.

Munickers!

It was a dodgy moment and the men exchanged acid looks. There would have been a row straight away only that one of the women smiled and acknowledged McCurtain's shabby joke with an equally shabby response. Pouting her glossy lips, she shifted around on the barstool and said they weren't half as tight as Dublin knickers.

McCurtain was taken aback, and after a moment's silence, everyone laughed it off. But he kept up his resentment. Wouldn't believe that the men were local.

You're not fuckin' Irish, he bawled. No way.

Bloody sure we are. York Road, born and bred.

Would you shag off! McCurtain waved his hand.

I swear to Jaysus. My passport has a fuckin' harp on it, you know.

But it was a big mistake to defend your origins in the Anchor Bar. McCurtain refused to accept their credentials. Challenged them to prove they were Irish by singing a song in the Irish language. And while McCurtain was looking the German women up and down with lascivious interest, the men sang *Cill Chais*. They got most of the words right and were clearly delighted at their excellent powers of retention. Working in a Bavarian printing firm with the noise of big machines around them every day, drinking abundant litres of German beer every night and still able to remember a sad old classroom lament to the ancient Irish oak forests. *Tá deire na gcoilte ar lár* . . . But even then, they didn't look Irish enough for McCurtain. I mean, how Irish do you have to be?

Krauts! You can't sing either.

Fuck off, one of them retorted. I'm as Irish as a Hiace van.

Ah! McCurtain exclaimed. Now why didn't you say that in the first place? At last he began to believe them. The Hiace van. A true icon of Irish life.

They shook hands and embraced each other like brothers. In turn, they called McCurtain a Hyundai hatchback, and everyone became instant friends. Hyundai and Hiace suddenly became more indigenous than the Irish themselves. More pints were called for, and there was laughter all around until one of the women suddenly slapped her hand on the bar counter and said she could not let it go. There was a point to be made here about the whole issue of ethnicity. Furious at the slur against her husband, the woman with the glossy lipstick laid the matter to rest once and for all with a short eloquent burst.

You fucking *Arschloch*, she said, pointing at McCurtain. What is this problem with you Irish? I don't care who is what here. And even if you are some kind of Celtic prince, you are still nothing but a big *Arschloch*.

Ah, take it easy, McCurtain said, holding his hands out in supplication.

The Anchor Bar was silent. The barmen stopped serving just to watch McCurtain being put in his place with a Bavarian *oomph*. She gunned him down with a big tirade while McCurtain looked at his shoes and leered. The twisted grin of shame.

Big Celtic *Arschloch!*

Coyne sat on his own with his pint, trowelling away the excess foam from his mouth with the back of his hand. The Anchor Bar was gaining momentum. Heading towards closing time fast. One of the visiting emigrants on the far side of the partition was still trying to put his origins beyond doubt with a new song. *You may travel far far, from your own native home*, he kept thrashing out again and again with fiery pride, but he couldn't really get going at all. The lyrics stopped there every time. Like a drunk trying to get up on a bike, cycling along with one foot but unable to swing his leg over the saddle and take off properly.

McCurtain wasn't going to listen to this philistine any longer. He spotted Coyne and went over to him. Bought him a double whiskey without even asking. Coyne was stunned at this generosity. What was happening? Had he won some money or something?

I hear you're dancing with strangers, McCurtain said.

Who?

Stranger came in here looking for you recently. Young Romanian supermodel.

How do you know?

Word of advice, Pat. Lay off the wet-backs, unless you want a visit.

Coyne laughed. The whiskey was placed on the counter beside his pint. A double Jameson. Ten years old and beaming through the glass with a reddish, gold glint. McCurtain threw out a fifty-pound note.

A visit from who? The Pope? Michael Jackson? Dana?

Look, I'm only the messenger, Pat. As a friend. Stay away from the strangers.

Shag off, Coyne said.

He turned on McCurtain. He was ready to put the Irish Casanova on his back. Nobody was going to tell Coyne who he could consort with. But there was something else behind this threat. Coyne looked at the whiskey on the counter, a strange contradiction of generosity and domination. What was this about a visit? Coyne knew what it meant. He was getting the hint, from a sacred organization. Coyne tried to counter the threat with cynicism. Imagined McCurtain going up to the Provo army council and saying: Lads, did you pay a visit yet?

What have you got to do with the Romanians?

Don't push your luck, Pat. I'm talking balaclavas here.

Coyne was vulnerable. He could fight McCurtain, but not the entire Provo hinterland. Maybe McCurtain had something to do with the poet getting beaten up outside the pub. Maybe McCurtain had something to do with Tommy Nolan. Everything was suitably enigmatic, and McCurtain's uncharacteristic generosity made Coyne think it was the end of freedom. What did it mean if Coyne accepted this drink?

Sláinte mhaith! McCurtain toasted.

Jesus, Coyne thought. Another closet Irish-speaker.

Coyne placed his hand around the poisoned chalice, rage and fear simultaneously taking hold of his motor neurons, while McCurtain smiled and nodded beside him. Coyne told himself not to be stupid. But he could not go along with the pretence. Instead of raising the glass up and tasting the precious drink of quiescence, Coyne turned it upside down on the counter. The alarming clack of glass on wood reached other customers. The barman looked up in horror, instinctively aware of that strained silence that presided over pre-violent moments of intense anger. People in the bar listened to all kinds of irrelevant, faraway sounds, like a car reversing at the back. The cooler shuddering. A shuffle of feet.

Smoke stood still. The Anchor Bar was a big lung holding its breath, ready to cough. Free molecules of single malt Jameson lifted into the air as Coyne stared straight ahead of him. His outstretched hand was still holding the glass, like a high-voltage fence, defying anyone to come and touch him as the whiskey slowly ran across the shiny surface of the counter, finding its own meandering course towards the ledge and dripping down at McCurtain's feet. Soaking into the dark, seasoned wood of the floorboards.

Coyne was back with the psychologist. This time Ms Dunford was determined to make some real progress and wanted more facts, stories. Anything that led the way back to Coyne's childhood where the underlying trauma lurked.

What has my childhood got to do with it? Coyne asked.

The fire has probably triggered off something in your memory.

No way! Coyne insisted. There's no bad memory. I'm clean.

She kept trying. There had to be some dirty childhood scandal somewhere. Nobody could even begin to sort themselves out until they went through all the historical stuff. OK. You didn't want to throw Coyne's identity out with the bad memories. But he would stumble through the rest of his life like a wounded animal if he didn't try to reconcile himself with it.

I can't remember a thing, he said. He gave the impression of a man who was firmly rooted in reality. His life was based on avoidance.

Ms Dunford was like a dog with a rubber femur. Snarling with Bonio excitement at the thought of discovery. She took a different angle.

Pat, you have a truth fixation.

Sure. I want the truth.

Yes, but you can't live with truth. We all live with symbols. We need dreams. Fiction.

She was pushing Coyne into a box. Next thing she would be asking him if he belonged to those who were afraid they were being watched during sex, or those who wanted to be watched during sex. Next thing she would be encouraging him to go back to work, like a child being forced back into a buggy and screaming in the street with stiff-backed resistance.

It's all about fantasy, she said. Lives are stories.

So?

The brain is basically a storyteller, she said. And maybe she was right, Coyne thought. Maybe the function of intelligence was to tell lies and detect lies. The Irish were such good liars. All that beautiful dishonesty. Force of history had made us into 'a craftie people'. Great storytellers with no resources but their imagination.

I'm not going to start spouting superlatives, Coyne declared.

Coyne's truth fixation centred on Carmel. He could see nothing but Carmel, corrupted by Hogan. He was blinded by her infidelity. He could see her leaning against the wall in Hogan's house. He could hear her little voice, the tiny gasp of pleasure that still resounded like a fading echo in Coyne's head. He was obsessed with that.

He thought of other stories in his life. He shuffled through the big data bank of dodgy memories. The bees killing his father. The language war. The hedgehog in the car. His own attempted suicide. The abandoned shoreline of Connemara. He searched through his childhood looking for big-time recovered memory.

I was put in the girls' class, he said finally. In primary school.

You remember being put in the girls' class, she echoed. As punishment.

Three times, Coyne said. Maybe more.

Ms Dunford took it seriously, though he expected her to show more astonishment. Maybe it wasn't the great character-breaking incident he'd always thought it was. Maybe all kids experienced some gender angst. At least Ms Dunford wasn't laughing at him. At least she didn't just dismiss it and say: We all went through that sort of thing. Toughened us up, emotionally.

What were you being punished for?

Coyne could not remember the crime involved. All he could remember was the punishment. They said he was a bold boy: *buachaill dána*. Then they dressed him up in ribbons and led him across the playground into the girls' school.

Yes, she encouraged. Go on.

Well, you know, he stammered. They brought me into the girls' class and put me sitting down. At the back of the class. Fourth class senior infants! *Rang a ceathar, cailíní*. The girls all kept looking around at me and laughing.

Ms Dunford tried not to smile. You poor thing, she wanted to say, put in there with all those girls. Humiliating. And terrifying too, I bet. Finally she was getting down to the real trauma. The Irish classroom. The austere rooms of childhood captivity, with high ceilings and cornice plaster-work. The grandeur of aristocratic homes, remodelled as Catholic schools in the new republic. All that bleak Georgian architecture of Dublin, casting a spell over innocent minds.

Do you equate women with punishment? she asked. Did this make you afraid of women?

No, not at all, Coyne said. I just wish they'd put me in a room with all of those *cailíní* now, wherever they are.

But that was sheer bravado. That was the small-boy macho line of defence he had always resorted to among his peers. The hero status he awarded himself when he was back with the boys again. Jesus, you don't know what you're missing, lads. You better do something really bad and get yourselves in there to *rang a ceathar, cailíní*. Underneath, Coyne was still trapped in the girl gulag, unable to get out. Unable to talk to women as equals. Still seeing everything in absolutes. Male and female. Black and white. Good and evil.

He recalled the fire. There was no fire brigade. Only neighbours running with buckets and basins. And children crowding on the pavement with bikes and rollerblades, stating the obvious in their own childish words. Look at the flames. Look at the mother screaming. There's a child left inside.

Coyne understood what was needed. The seconds were critical. He wrapped a wet coat around his arm and burst through the front door. His final act in uniform. He ran into a wall of smoke and toxic fumes behind which he saw the stripes of yellow flame and heard the growl of crackling wood.

I remember shouting, Coyne said. As though he could frighten the inferno off with his rage. Pushing through the smoke and punching at the flames. Choking and coughing until his lungs seemed to burst. His arms and knees felt the sharp stab of heat, as the anger of the fire turned on him. Coyne on his own. Just blind heroism.

He reached the return, halfway up the stairs. People were shouting at him not to go any further. The stairs were about to collapse. He stood on a mass of gleaming red cinders, as though the floor beneath him had been eaten away by red and black ants. Thousands of them with their red-hot pincers. In his urgency, Coyne had put his foot right down and felt the wood shifting underfoot, biting through his shoe. Hundreds of them gnawing through the leather at once.

His eyes were flooding with tears and smoke. He could not see a thing. Blindly lashing about him and shouting. Making one more effort to disperse the smoke and see up towards the landing. Because he heard a voice. And then momentarily saw the child at the top of the stairs crying, before his feet gave way. The cinder ants had eaten through the supports. The entire staircase collapsed underneath him. It was too late. He fell back down and his colleague dragged him out again on to the lawn.

That's what Coyne remembered. The endless loop of heroic failure. The sadness of defeat. The sound of voices all around him. And the rage of the fire taking over, given new life with a draught of wind gusting through the house, from the front door to the back window. Glass panes bursting in the heat.

Ms Dunford suggested psycho-drama again, getting together with a group of other wackoes so that Coyne could re-enact his traumatic moments. She was getting excited about the idea. Jumped up from her swivel chair and started plodding around the room in her big webbed feet again. Put her hands on Coyne's shoulders and gently pushed him back in his seat when he attempted to get up and escape.

Relax, she said. I'm not going to do anything to you.

Then she waddled around the room again.

I have an idea, she began. *Vergangenheitsbewältigung!*

What? Coyne moved back in his seat when her face came close to his. He was afraid of this new fiction. Give me back my truth fixation.

Why don't we bring you back to that school. Why don't we turn you into a little boy again. Just for one day.

Are you serious?

Why don't we put you in short trousers and bring you back?

You mean physically go back?

Yes! Why not?

Jesus Christ! Coyne should never have opened his mouth. Now look what he was getting himself into. An encounter with the past. Back to the classrooms of fear. Sitting in with the *cailíní*, just to see what effect it had on his psyche. You must be joking, Dunford.

The Anchor Bar was closed for renovations. Coyne was hoping to do a little group therapy with McCurtain and went around some of the other bars looking for him. McCurtain had some questions to answer.

In the meantime, Coyne started re-enacting all his own gear-grinding memories. Raking over his childhood with an increasingly reductive menace which was either going to destroy him or funnel him out through a gateway of pastoral calmness perhaps. For the moment, it was doing nothing but damage. The fire had taken hold of his intellect, standing out as the leading symbol of all his losses. Cuckold. Failure. Burglary victim. A cumulative powerlessness driving him on a self-destructive mission.

Somebody had to pay for this. It had worked before. Direct action!

Coyne phoned Killjoy once more, this time just bawling a string of abuse down the line, all about Killjoy's wife Nora. It was the only way to make Killjoy wake up and take notice.

It was time to put a few things right in this town: not just Killmurphy, but Hogan as well. The man who wrecked his dreams and blasphemed against his erotic mythology.

As he walked up towards Hogan's house, Coyne swept

through the full traumatic economy of his existence. All the landmarks of hurt and defeat. Starting with the beige door of his school, going through all the wars and arguments in his life, all the way up to the fire that had put him out of work. The crackling fury of the red cinders under his feet. The victorious laughter of the fire and the hollow apology of his own static inadequacy. He could visualize Carmel's transgression with Hogan. Her breasts offered up to Hogan's eyes like an exotic confection, the forward thrust design of the green bra exaggerating the gift-wrapped effect. A coy gaze downwards to undo the bow at the back and allow the harness to float away freely. And Hogan's boyish hands testing the spontaneous white Plasticine bounce of her emancipated breasts. The blind curiosity of his thumbs slipping across her illuminated nipples.

After all, Coyne knew her body so well: a territorial knowledge that was all the more vivid for the intrusive gaze. Hogan was looking in, disturbing the phantasmal secrecy of his love for Carmel. Bastard voyeur! Peeping into Coyne's dreams. Shattering the frail intensity of his sexual illusion.

He found himself marching towards Hogan's mansion – a land agitator finally driven by the limits of endurance to confront his landlord. Some kind of attack on his person or property is what Coyne intended. He didn't care what appalling ramifications would ensue. It was an act of passion. Of moral justice.

Along the way, Coyne passed by a building site and saw an earthmover parked quietly in a little compound. A corporation JCB which belonged to the new South Dublin sewerage scheme. They had spent months drilling through the granite crust of the earth under Dublin Bay, laying concrete pipes in order to carry Hogan's precious little nuggets of personal waste out to sea. It was time to move the earth under Hogan's feet. Just watch Coyne arriving on the doorstep with this JCB. There would be no time to cut the ribbon on the big sewerage scheme. No time to get to the bathroom even. Hogan would experience an embarrassing little solid accident in his trousers.

There were no witnesses. Coyne got into the cab of the JCB, hot-wired the starting motor with a bent nail and drove out straight across a plywood hoarding with shocking force. No need to open the gate. Such liberation! Such triumphant empowerment of the underclasses! It had the democratic mandate of a rebel song. The man who drove this egalitarian vehicle had the ability to change not only the face of the earth, but the course of history too. No earthly obstacles could impede the onrush of inevitability. Coyne, the revolutionary, driving steadily around the corner until he could see the stone lions coming into view. This was a poetic strike. The JCB chugged along the coast road like a dinosaur. A giant T-Rex making its way towards the home of Councillor Sylvester Hogan with primordial vengeance.

Coyne saw the pebbled driveway and the cluster of three birch trees on the lawn. For Christsake, he thought. That's a real give-away, Hogan. That's nearly as bad as the three ducks on the wall, you fecking *leibide*.

Coyne had now mastered the lifting gear. The T-Rex was opening his mouth and growling with voracious intent as he headed for the stone guardians. One lurching mechanical movement forward was all it took to lift each of them into the air. The lion on the left had an indifferent plastercast expression on his face as though he was about to ignore this great prehistoric predator and continue peacefully licking his own balls. The dinosaur moved through the gateway and towards the house, crashing right through the big bay window with the ruched curtains and spitting the animal out in disgust on the living-room carpet with a huge crescendo of breaking glass. When the JCB reversed, there seemed to be even more noise as it pulled the buckled PVC window frames out with it, lurching back and forth a little to maximize the destruction. Coyne then drove back for the other lion, which yawned imperviously as Coyne delivered him on to the doorstep of Hogan's home.

Coyne parked the T-Rex in the porch, taking one of the Ionic pillars down with him and breaking through the front door into the hallway before jumping down from the JCB and walking away. A primitive parable. He was sorry he couldn't stay and look at the disaster in more detail. But he carried with him the image of the lion on his back in the living room, surrounded by glass, the heavy velvet curtains moving in the breeze and the tangled PVC bay window frames lying in the rose bed. The JCB with its nose embedded in the front door.

Good lad, he said to himself. Give that man a doughnut.

As he walked away along the seafront, he seemed to be followed by a big cheer of appreciation, the roar of a football stadium. Coyne the suburban terrorist.

The lights came on in Hogan's house. Hogan and his wife came out and stood at the front door in slippers surveying the damage, appalled and horrified. Beyond belief. The moral outrage meter returning all Hogan's troubles at once. He was suffering from an acute form of back pain. A painful tingling around the back of his thigh, as though he and his long-suffering wife, St Norma of the waxed bikini line, were doing some kind of sciatica waltz on the doorstep.

Mongi O Doherty was in a particularly asexual mood that evening. Having gone back to visit Sharon, the woman in his life most likely to represent carnal solace and least likely to fulfil a role in domestic economy, he was now curiously uninterested in sex. What he really needed was a mother who could cook, play the sex kitten, offer Oedipal comfort and also give breathtaking advice on business matters. As well as shut up and stay out of sight from time to time.

Sharon was a lousy cook; but she was all over Mongi with affection and sweetness, full of Rose of Tralee kindness.

Her palliative, chimebox voice got a bit stifling at times, because all Mongi wanted to do that evening was to lie around bollock naked and watch football. Above him, the festooned canopy of the bed with its peach lace drapes hanging down like two half-moons. It was one of the last games on the soccer calendar. A testimonial, he called it. And what could be more unerotic than end of season, drag on, scoreless draw football. The referee hadn't even produced a yellow card yet.

Sharon was doing her best to liven up the situation, instantly assuming that there was something wrong with her if her partner preferred soccer. She was practically maiming herself. Trying to wrap her legs around one of the mahogany poles at the foot of the bed, vaulting across the massive TV in a red, cheese-cutter thong and recklessly reversing her centre-spread backside into his face, without even as much as a blink from Mongi.

I can't fuckin' see! You're blocking my view, he said. Sharon sulked.

Sport was the end of imagination. It was a refuge from sexuality and engagement. A mushroom cloud of sterility. She could tell by the heartburn look of bitterness on his face that he was not even satisfied by the game. He was gnawing like a badger at his already depleted fingernails, and it looked like the only thing he wanted to do with Sharon was to start biting her false purple-black talons. He was self-absorbed. He had failed to get his hands on Jimmy Coyne. In addition to that, he had been questioned by the cops in relation to the murder of Tommy Nolan. Sergeant Corrigan had put a number of awkward scenarios to him earlier on at his mother's house while his hamburger was going cold.

Sergeant Corrigan was now presenting Mongi with all the evidence he had collected. Amazing the amount of witnesses he had found. Mongi was a cornered rat, ran the theme of his message. And the Gardai were thematic, schematic bastards. There was only one thing Mongi hated more than all this unwanted attention, and that was being called by his real name, Richard. Pronounced by Sergeant Corrigan as Rigid! Spoiled his appetite and fucked up all his *jouissance*.

To make matters worse, Sharon started talking to Mongi's mickey. Mongi thought he was hearing things. Addressing his pecker, she was, in dulcet, nursery tones. She knelt down and had a private conversation with it as if Mongi didn't exist and this floppy little instrument of power and pleasure was the only friend she had in the world. As though Mongi's half-stiff ego was located right there in his ragdoll member. Careful not to get in the way of the lacklustre images of soccer, she chatted away.

Come here, my little pet! What's the matter with you tonight, you poor little peckerhead?

At first, Mongi ignored the use of these diminutive adjectives. All lovable items were little to the women he knew. A nurturing instinct to reduce everything to manageable infant dependency. A Sindy doll universe. Venerating his fragile id, kissing it and shaking it playfully from side to side, trying to spark a debate against the background noise of indifferent football cheers. Until she used one Lilliput superlative too many.

My sweet little sprat, she said, nudging it with her nose and whimpering.

Mongi looked down and discovered that his mickey had indeed taken on the blue-green stripes of a lower infant class mackerel. Flapping about and hyperventilating like it was out of water in an over-oxygenated environment.

What did you call it?

Darling little sprat, she repeated, looking up at Mongi with great concern. It was the wrong word. She tried to swallow and withdraw her face.

Too late! Mongi lifted her with a punch in the mouth that sent her across the room. There was a neat, audible click of her lips as the fist made contact. A wasted string of libidinal saliva was left hanging in the air and Mongi wiped his knuckles on the bedspread in distaste. Then he jumped up and grabbed a lamp in the shape of a black nude bearing a yellow globe on her shoulder. Held it like a joystick, took Sharon by the hair and threatened to electrocute her womb if she ever used that term again.

You're saying it smells like a fish! he shouted.

No! Jesus, Mongi. I didn't say that.

You insinuated that I'm a fishmonger.

Mongi, no! Please. I swear!

Sharon was shaking. Her lipstick had turned to blood. She was astonished by the level of aggression involved in the preamble to sex these days. Thug foreplay. A bit of rough. A multi-pack of bruised breast fantasies delivered in one terrifying domestic assault. Gratified only by the stuttering sound of her Rose of Tralee voice begging for mercy, he switched off the TV, ready to punish this grievous misappellation.

Never say sprat again.

I promise, Mongi, she whispered, white in face. Counting her teeth with a scarlet tongue. Please don't mark me.

He kissed her mouth and sucked her swollen lip. Mongi the vampire, swallowing the taste of terror. But in that moment, the cellular phone rang. After him getting all worked up for it, then came the crass intrusion of the mobile phone. Another setback. An urgent business development that put an instant dampener on Mongi's dark desire. It was Jack McCurtain. A serious problem had arisen in the wet-back situation.

Of course. Why hadn't Coyne thought of this earlier? If McCurtain had been chosen to deliver a paramilitary message to Coyne, then he had to be in a position to lead the way. They expected Coyne to be afraid, they expected him to shrivel. Like all those people who had their windows painted black in final warning. They thought he would be cowering in his flat at the mention of balaclavas. Coyne felt vulnerable at first. Any man with a family would. But he had nothing to lose any more. He would not fret for the rest of his life like a frightened rabbit. Not Coyne.

He found McCurtain's house, rang the bell and waited. The door opened and emitted a waft of curry. McCurtain saw Coyne and instantly tried to slam the door. Like they used to slam the door shut on all the Mormons and Latter-day Saints and Poppy Day sellers. Feck off back to England. Anyone that didn't conform with Catholic republican ideals. Coyne's own father was the same, slamming the door so the whole street would shake.

McCurtain didn't care for any creed at his door after midnight. He whacked the door like a tennis racket, creating a hostile gust in the hallway. The rebuff on the Irish doorstep. Except that Coyne was too fast an opponent. Stuck his itinerant boot in the door, close to the hinge at the angle of least resistance. Caused the door to bounce back ineffectually.

Sorry to disturb your dinner, Coyne said.

I'm busy.

You shouldn't be eating that kind of stuff so late at night. Give you nightmares.

What do you want?

I'm looking for your friend, the man with the mackerel.

Listen, it's got nothing to do with me. I don't take moral responsibility for anything else. I'm only the messenger, Coyne.

The dove from above, is that it?

Coyne pushed his way into the house and closed the door behind him. The smell of bindi bhaji was overpowering. He pushed McCurtain along the hallway towards the kitchen where he had been eating his take-away and watching hardcore porn. Tarka dhal and simultaneous ejaculations. For Christsake! Coyne was not easily disgusted by other people's proclivities, unless they included golf. But the

146

thought of McCurtain horsing into his erotic Indian dinner was a sight too far. Indian food was the pornography of world cuisine.

Where is he? Coyne shouted.

Who?

The bastard with the message.

McCurtain claimed he had no way of contacting him. It was all operating on a strict cell system now.

Coyne had had enough of this evasion. Grabbed him by the neck and pushed him back into a chair, so that McCurtain suddenly found himself reclining gracefully with his legs sticking out straight for balance. Arms flailing around trying to grab hold of his take-away and sending basmati all over the kitchen floor.

For one minute, McCurtain thought he could get out of this by force. He got his hands on a fork and started stabbing the back of Coyne's neck, like some Jurassic bird pecking, until Coyne threw him down and cracked his head on the terracotta tiled floor.

Coyne felt his neck. Like a zip had been opened, letting in the air. His hand was red. The television was making appropriate gasping sounds of agony.

McCurtain, you Casanova bastard. You shouldn't have done that.

McCurtain huddled in the corner with his fork. Tried to gouge Coyne's eye out this time, until he was dispossessed of his weapon. There followed a straight, *Ryan's Daughter* style punch-up in the kitchen. McCurtain at times gaining the upper hand, throwing tarka dhal straight into Coyne's eyes. But at last Coyne won the battle and pinned McCurtain to the floor with the chair.

You're forcing me to do this, Coyne said.

He took a bottle of Tabasco sauce and stuck it up McCurtain's nose. A jet of the fiery liquid made its way down the nostril, burning through McCurtain's sinuses, making him sneeze half a dozen times in quick succession.

147

This was chemical warfare. Red-hot lava trickling around the nasal cavity more powerful than any caustic toilet cleaner.

I swear, I don't know!

Another squirt of Tabasco in McCurtain's eye caused him to weep convulsively. Red-eye McCurtain, crying for Ireland. His eyeball bathing in a socket of acid. It was the only way of dealing with the situation, the physical force tradition. Fighting fire with fire. The inherent paradox of all warfare. Violence to end all violence.

Wait! McCurtain shouted at last. Can I make a phone call?

Mongi was furious. Right in the middle of a delicate moment in the build-up to love he had to negotiate with McCurtain. Jesus, the pong of garlic coming down the phone line was enough to put him off sex, if not football as well, for a year.

McCurtain was trying to speak in code. Explained his predicament in the most eloquent Irish. *Tá mé i sáin*, he said, using a common chess analogy. By the grimace on his face, it looked like McCurtain had surrendered.

Have you ever wondered what happens after checkmate? Coyne asked. The game doesn't end there. Tell that to your friend. The next move is even more interesting. The defeated king gets roasted alive in a cauldron of Tabasco sauce.

Mongi put the statuesque bedside lamp of the black nude on the floor as he listened to this arcane gibberish coming at him across the phone in the middle of the night.

Gabh' agus fuckáil thú féin, he said.

Mongi didn't care about McCurtain. Why should he care if this ex-cop gave McCurtain a hiding. Let him give McCurtain the vindaloo treatment. They would get Coyne back in good time.

Meigeal an Mhaighdean Mhuire, McCurtain was screaming. He'll kill me.

Coyne started laughing to himself. What was all this garlic lark. Didn't they know that Coyne was a fluent Irish speaker? Coyne the true native. Not like these half arsed Irish speakers who spread a patina of the language all over the country like low-cholesterol margarine. Abusing the mother-tongue, turning it into an incendiary device. Gaelic as a weapon of war.

Coyne grabbed the phone from McCurtain and spoke directly to the leader.

Listen here, *a mhac*, Coyne shouted. Those new visitors from Romania. They're my friends. If you ever lay a finger on them again I'll incinerate your pal here. Every grain of that basmati rice is going into his urethra. Then I'll come over to your place and do the same to you, mate.

Mongi was calm. His fury had not had enough time to percolate into his nerve endings, still tingling with sexual promise. In the background, Sharon was tousling her hair. Exaggerating a rip in her belly-top and lying back as though she'd just been knocked off a horse or a tractor. Simulating a farming accident: absentmindedly taking blood from her mouth and smearing it on her cheeks. On her left ear.

Stop that, Mongi barked at her.

Coyne burst into another poetic string of golden Irish treasures. Cursing at Mongi with real *blas*. Mongi could not help being impressed. *Beidh tú sínte, a mhac, le bud asail I do bheal agus méar an deabhail I do thóin*. Coyne was advising Mongi to put his mackerel in his mouth and smoke it.

Diúg do roinneach.

Mongi responded with a few lacklustre expletives and threw the phone across the room. What was the point in talking to this crazed native speaker?

Mongi sat back on the bed. He had no real interest in the language, except for its fetish value And there was no way that he could resume the intensity of his love for Sharon, after all that garlic. Not with the same sadistic brio. He looked down and saw that his mickey had been reduced to a minnow. Paucity pecker! It was money he was thinking of. Because there was nothing as erotic as money. He was thinking hard.

Coyne found himself on shaky emotional ground after the encounter, as though there was some benign hand laid on his shoulder by the Irish language that made him tolerant again. Those few words made him realize what he had been missing. That sense of lost friendship. The consensus in adversity. Now at last he knew what was wrong with his country. They had lost that close-knit sense of support and good will towards each other when things were poor and everyone spoke Irish.

McCurtain was snivelling and nursing his eye while Coyne was struck by a huge wave of remorse. It was an unforgivable thing to do, to interfere with a man's meal.

It was just like the bread and seagulls incident where Tommy Nolan dropped his sandwiches in the school-yard and let out a silent shout of pain.

I'm sorry about that, Coyne said. It's not right.

What? McCurtain said, looking up with fear, still coughing and spitting.

I want to apologize for doing this to your food. I didn't mean to. It was wrong.

McCurtain was amazed by the sudden kindness and didn't trust such a dramatic personality change. He wished Coyne would stop talking about the food. Leave it alone. The damage was done now.

Can I get you some more rice? Coyne asked. Look, I'll go down and get anything you want. I feel terrible about this.

But it was too late. The Indian take-away was already shut. McCurtain gazed in astonishment at this bizarre reversal as Coyne picked up the grains of rice one by one. Coyne straightened up the chair. Swore he would make up for it as he lifted McCurtain up and ushered him towards the table, begging him to resume his meal. Hoping to Christ he still had his appetite.

Here, have some more of this bindi bhaji. I didn't touch it.

There was remorse in the air. Skipper Martin Davis was also feeling a deep new unspeakable guilt on account of the death of Tommy Nolan. Even though he had no part in his death, he still felt he had contributed with his presence, with his words and with his tacit support. The force-feeding incident with the mackerel had changed his mind and he was now hoping to erect some kind of memorial to Tommy Nolan. He began to make a collection. Or effectively a bogus collection, because very few people could spare more than a few pence for a memorial and it was Martin Davis himself who put up the money. Then he consulted McCurtain, the guru of all commemoration, to see how best it could be set up. Perhaps some kind of plaque outside Tommy's council flat, or somewhere at the harbour, near to where he died. But that was a little too close for comfort, perhaps. They discussed the idea of a brass plate at the Anchor Bar, to show public appreciation for what Tommy had meant in their society.

Sergeant Corrigan was up early, standing on an outcrop of rock, looking out to sea through a pair of Garda binoculars. The lenses were a bit blurred, but he could see the *Lolita* just out beyond the bay, returning with a catch of fish and the trailing seagulls. What mystified him was that skipper Martin Davis had so suddenly decided to return to fishing. With the blue sky of an early summer's day, he was out there in the Irish Box hauling in the first mackerel shoal of the season, listening to them slapping about in the hold.

If the binoculars had been any stronger, Corrigan would have detected a smile of plain pleasure on Martin Davis's face as he sang to himself through his beard. Belly to the breeze. With the seagull chant in the background, the drone of the engine underneath him and the swell of the sea lifting the boat like the chorus of a song, he was reverting to a simple lifestyle. An ancient devotion to the sea. There was nothing to beat the frenzied sight of fish throwing themselves helplessly on deck in their thousands. Multitudes of green-blue mackerel. Better than the sight of money.

Coyne was on his own in the flat. He hadn't seen Jimmy in days. Since the big incident on the pier, his son had disappeared.

Coyne was decapitating a late morning boiled egg. Many people would have expected him to regret what he had done. To feel fear. To acknowledge some sense of impending reckoning for taking on the might of Mongi O Doherty. There was a lot of unfinished business out there.

Instead, Coyne was in a fighting mood. Shouting at the radio again.

Good, he roared, when the news broke that an oil company drilling off the west coast had failed to discover any commercial yields. After initially positive indications from geologists, shareholders had their hopes dashed. Disaster! A spokesman for the company said they would be exploring further sites, but that the field closest to the Aran Islands had sadly proved uncommercial.

Well, I'm glad, Coyne shouted back at the radio.

Jaysus, the country was in a state of bereavement. Flags should be flying at half mast and Coyne was laughing. Great news. One last reprieve! Leave that fucking oil where it is, you bastards.

There was a knock on the door. He was in the middle of his tirade, pointing a lump of egg yolk at the radio. Squinting with hot idealism at the invisible oil spokesman as though he was going to kill him with a spoon. He stood up and went to the door.

Carmel.

Somebody had let her in at the hall door. Maybe Coyne hadn't heard the bell with all the shouting.

Great, Coyne thought at first. Finally, she had decided to visit him. He asked her to come inside and sit down. She had ignored her mother's warnings. Into the den of thieves. But there was something solemn about the way Carmel stood in the middle of the room and looked down in disgust at the frugal egg on the table. Smell of toast in the air. One of his familiar T-shirts on the radiator. And a colourful kiddies plaster stuck on the back of his neck.

I'll never forgive you, she said, tears in her eyes.

What? Coyne with his schoolboy innocence.

What you did to that man's lions.

What lions?

You know very well what I'm talking about, Pat. It's disgraceful. Destroying his home like that. And for what?

Coyne reached over to the top of the fridge and grabbed a feckless amount of tissues out of the box. Handed them to Carmel. Jesus, she was starting to cry and Coyne would not know what to do then.

Don't expect me to get you out of this, she said. You can go to jail for this one, I don't care. I never want to speak to you again. So you needn't come up to the house. You can talk to Mr Fennelly.

Carmel had threatened the solicitor before, but this seemed more serious. She moved towards the door and opened it so that all his neighbours could hear his most intimate affairs. She wanted the public on her side.

You've nothing to say for yourself, have you?

Carmel, please. Sit down.

Piss off, she said. Doing a thing like that. And you've no explanation, have you. Because you're full of spite and jealousy. You're full of hate.

Carmel, look!

You're nothing but a vandal. A civic disaster. It's an abomination.

This was a smear campaign. She had no evidence that Coyne drove the T-Rex into Hogan's house. She was just making a wild assumption. Totally unfair.

Don't smear me, he appealed.

Besides, any fucking eejit with lions on his gatepost deserved to be dismembered and devoured in a Colosseum of plastercast artefacts. An audience of garden gnomes grinning at him and an eternity in the kitsch kingdom of hell at the end of it. With Christy Hennessey singing in his ear twenty-four hours a day. What about all those Toblerone cottages in Achill Island. What about that for a civic disaster?

You've nothing to say for yourself, Carmel said bitterly. Do you realize that poor man has a very bad back. He was just starting to respond to therapy. Showing great signs of improvement. And now look what you've done. He's virtually an invalid with all the pain.

Brilliant, Coyne wanted to say.

You've ruined his life.

It's you and me, Coyne said at last. But it was the wrong moment entirely. The timing was atrocious. Instead of showing some modicum of contrition, he was now going in the wrong direction altogether. He was in another world and could not connect with her anger. He was more inclined to start singing a cheap new love song to her. Let's get it on, baby. It's you and me, maybe. Lovers keep on loving – darling keep on pushing – 'cause I'm gonna keep on gushing!

She looked at Coyne as though he was completely heartless. Have you no feeling?

At that moment she saw the rock on the mantelpiece: the rock with the white Saturn ring which had mysteriously gone missing from her room one day. There it was now in

Coyne's flat, like a piece of her life that he had misappropriated and kept hidden. She looked at the stone, then back at Coyne. Fury and sadness in her eyes at the same time, knowing that she would always be stuck with him in some way or another.

She threw the tissues in his direction and turned to leave. They floated towards him and down to the floor, descending gradually like individual feathers. His reaction was to try at all costs to prevent any of them from reaching the floor. Grabbing and clutching at them while she ran out the door and down the stairs.

We're inextricably linked! he shouted after her. Neighbours downstairs looking up in disbelief and nervous curiosity.

Sergeant Corrigan was taking an even more grim view, standing at Coyne's door later the same day with a sombre look on his face. As a colleague and a local Garda ambassador, as an impartial agent of justice and a father of two boys himself, it was his painful duty to take Jimmy in for questioning once again.

This might come as a bit of a shock to you, Corrigan said. But we have reason to believe that your son has taken some kind of revenge act on Mr Hogan. With a bulldozer.

Coyne chuckled at the glittering irony of this accusation. Once again they had levelled at the child the crimes of his forefathers. Blame and moral responsibility passed on like a genetic inheritance. An heirloom of guilt and knock-on atonement.

He's not here, Coyne answered. And I don't believe he would have done a thing like that. Jimmy's changed.

I'm afraid he'll have to answer a few questions, Corrigan insisted.

I don't even know where he is. Haven't seen him for days. Weeks.

You'll only make matters worse.

Sergeant Corrigan sympathized with the fact that Coyne would want to back up his son. But it was better not to push a man with Whistler's reputation to the limit. This was a criminal investigation. He would be back.

Coyne suddenly changed the subject altogether. It was the only thing to do. Just as Corrigan was about to leave in frustration, he dropped a crucial cultural test.

Do you mind if I ask you a personal question, Coyne said.

Go ahead.

Did you watch *Forrest Gump* last night?

Yeah! Great movie, Corrigan said without reservation. Marvellous!

Thousands of people had watched the film on TV and the country was already divided into polarized camps – those who thought it was great and those who thought it was complete and utter rubbish. The same old breakdown of affinities. Except that from now on everything boiled down to what side of the Gump divide you were on.

I thought it was crap, Coyne eventually said with a grin.

Corrigan was shocked. He took it personally. Lashed back from his mono-cultural barricade and told Coyne he was going to be in trouble.

One of these fine days I'll sort you out, he warned.

But Coyne was smiling with elitist superiority. Corrigan raised his eyebrows. As far as he was concerned, Coyne was the odd man out. The loser. The uncool heretic who didn't get the message.

Jimmy was hiding out with Nurse Boland in her small, top of the house flat overlooking the seafront. His life had been syncopated into a timeless fantasy; the spatio-temporal vacuum of a high Georgian love nest with tall ceilings and large sash windows going from knee height right up to the ceiling. Every day, when Irene went out to work, he looked out over the blue sea and watched the ferry appearing on the horizon, enjoying the langourous repetition of people parking their cars and getting out to walk along the promenade towards the pier. Summer clothes were coming back at last. Buckets and spades. Children going swimming and playing ball along the waterfront. Dogs running in circles and figures of eight.

Jimmy Coyne and Irene Boland had struck a rich vein of bliss. He would never have to leave that apartment again. Every night she nursed his fractured ankle. Bathing it, drying it carefully, rubbing ointment into the swollen, purple stain around his foot and mummifying it in a new binding. After which they made love and danced and loved and drank and took their drugs.

He missed the Haven nursing home. He missed shaving old men and speeding down the long lino corridor with the wheelchairs. Acting the fool with residents. Cracking jokes and doing interpretations of Coolio or James Brown in front of them. Instead, he undertook the housekeeping at the flat, hoovering and dusting and cleaning the big windows; even tackling the sticky, salt-encrusted stains of spring storms on the outside, so that when Irene came home she thought there was no glass at all, they were so clear. He discovered a natural talent for cooking; started producing some magnificent Italian masterpieces. Goat's cheese lasagne! Mushroom and Stilton risotto. Homemade spinach ravioli. As they sat over dinner in the evening, looking out at the solitary cargo ships moored in the black bay, he talked about getting married and going to live in Italy with her.

I have money, he said. Loads of money.

I'm nearly twice your age, she argued.

So? Why should that matter?

He stood naked at the window in the dark, with his skinny white body and his bony backside, making up stories while she sat in the armchair behind him, all bulbous and plump. They were a perfect couple as long as they remained in hiding and eluded their pursuers. Like Diarmuid and Gráinne.

They're after me, Jimmy said. We have to go away. They're going to kill me.

She laughed at the way he announced this threat with such gravity, as though she had anticipated this sex-induced paranoia. He had begun to invent a kind of fugitive mythology; a beleaguered mindset that became an essential part of their relationship. Love was not possible without these vital ingredients of fear and forced exile.

They're going to kill me, he said at least once every day, like a mantra.

It provided a context of ending. Of exclusion. A terminal narrative in which every moment was stolen. They were living with a fatwa.

Coyne took on the role of tour guide one afternoon. He had promised to show Corina and some of her Romanian friends around Trinity College and other landmarks of the city. He talked to them about the famous writers. About historical facts. Here and there he stopped and told them about a bank raid, giving them the exact details, with dates of arrests and convictions. In some instances he was able to tell them the calibre of weapons used and the number of shots fired. He gave them a legal tour of the city – fraud cases, murders, abductions. It was all told with great enthusiasm, as if Dublin was famous for its crime. As he brought them up towards Stephen's Green he had something to say about every shop and every building. He stopped and gave them a brief history of the State. It was not unlike the Soviet Union.

Worse, Coyne said. At one time, every Irish child had an invisible listening device planted in its head.

Corina laughed.

Marlene Nolan was contacted by a number of people from

the Anchor Bar in connection with a memorial plaque which they wanted to erect. It was explained to her that some of the fishermen including Martin Davis had made a collection to honour Tommy Nolan at the newly refurbished, soon to be reopened, Anchor Bar. McCurtain had been appointed treasurer and spokesman, so he called on Marlene to hammer out the wording at her small corporation flat. The place was blue with smoke. TV on at ten in the morning: another documentary on the death of Diana.

I don't know what to put on it, she appealed.

She was not used to this kind of decision. The power of words had always been the domain of the Catholic Church, poets and politicians.

What do you think Tommy would like? McCurtain asked.

But it was not what Tommy might have wanted, so much as what the community wanted. Some phrase or sentiment had to be found that would expiate their guilt. Like a candle in the wind. A local deification process by which the victim was becoming a contemporary saint and martyr, raised to the status of suburban hero. Not because of anything he did in his awkward, uneventful life, but because of the way in which his life ended. The people of this coastal Dublin borough needed to raise his memory out of the dirty harbour water in which he had drowned. Tommy Nolan, up there along with Princess Diana and Bobby Sands.

Here sat Tommy. Here sat Tommy and drank his pint. In memory of Tommy Nolan who was a regular here.

McCurtain was looking for something more legendary and dignified. Marlene smoked a dozen cigarettes trying to think, but her words seemed too crass: May the man who sits on this seat never be short of the price of a pint. May God bless Tommy Nolan. Even the old religious invocations sounded trite and misplaced in a pub.

McCurtain suggested a line from a song. *Four Green Fields*, he thought would have had a good, resonant line in it, so he quickly went through the lyrics to see if anything stood out, half singing or speed reciting his way through it. In the end, she picked something from Tommy's favourite number. *Three wheels on my wagon, and I'm still rolling along. The Cherokees are after me. . . .*

Perfect! At last, with tears in her eyes, Marlene made up her mind. It was the ideal way to describe Tommy with his limp, as though he'd always been missing a wheel or two but still managed to keep going. The symbolism was right. *I'm still rolling along!*

Clare Dunford was of the opinion that Coyne would profit from a session under hypnosis. Perhaps something would emerge that Coyne had suppressed all his life.

You can try all you like, he said. I can't be hypnotized. I'm not the type to yield under pressure.

If you'll allow me, she said, smiling. We can take it from there.

You're wasting your time, he argued. My personality isn't taken in by a dangling watch. Besides, I'm too much on edge. I'd never be relaxed enough.

Just let me try, she said.

Go ahead, he said. Be my guest, but it's not going to work.

Ms Dunford pushed him gently back in his seat, trying to disarm him. But the softness of her approach made him even more tense and hostile, determined not to slip into her power. He had become an expert at resistance. Insurrection. Repulsion.

She suddenly changed her style and began to turn Coyne's inner defiance into an advantage.

You're trying to resist me, she said, looking right into his eyes. You're really concentrating hard on staying awake, aren't you? You're using all your energy to counteract mine.

And finally he succumbed to her commanding tone, or perhaps it was more to her teeth, which forced him to imagine that he was floating upside down in the room. He was soon spilling out all kinds of debris from his cluttered mind, like an attic of stored memorabilia, a Gothic novel of psycho-babble.

The dogs of illusion, he repeated over and over. First he went into confessional mode, revealing a range of misdeeds that took Dunford by surprise. Then he began to rail against his enemies. He was cursing and swearing in the most vicious language known to man. *Téigh g'an deabhaill!*

By suggestion, Ms Dunford lightly steered him away and began to probe a little deeper to see if there was a more passive Coyne underneath. What she found was a benevolent maniac, because Coyne instantly snapped over into a phase of generosity in which everyone became his best friend. He was spouting superlatives.

Marvellous. I think you're all bloody fantastic, he said. Magnificent.

Dunford was alarmed at this sudden transformation. He was lashing out hysterical blandishments and hugging the world with new optimism. He was positively sentimental, full of cheap good will and gleaming TV commercial virtues.

It was a worrying development. She had unlocked Coyne's head and watched him descend into a spate of uncontained adulation, sitting in the chair and waving his hand about like a pontiff, giving his blessing to all. His fighting exterior had concealed a vulnerable intellect, given to bouts of indiscriminate praise. Beneath all the aggression and dereliction she found a vulnerable boy. He was a walking paradox, a victim-oppressor, an exhibitionist and a shy recluse, a mess of contradictions ready to switch over at any moment to benign pathos.

We are all bloody great, he announced. We are the best in the world. Nobody can match us. The rest of the bastards are only trotting after us.

Dunford could not bear it any longer and clicked her

fingers. Coyne snapped out of his trance looking unusually relaxed.

Bet you I didn't say anything, he said cheerfully.

Ms Dunford would not respond at first, as though she was afraid to reveal the truth.

I knew it, he laughed triumphantly. I wouldn't break under torture either.

I'm afraid you did, Pat.

What? Coyne sat up. Eyes open. What did I say?

You started praising everything in sight, she told him. You said everything was good.

No way, Coyne barked. You're making this up.

He sat back again, obviously distressed. Betrayed by the Coyne within. There was nothing he could do about it.

I think it would be good idea to go back to the school, she suggested.

It won't do any good, he said.

She came over and put her hand on his shoulder.

Coyne went to visit the grave of his mother that same afternoon. No matter what crisis might arise, he could not miss going to the cemetery on her anniversary.

It was his mother he thought of first. He could hardly remember his father's death, it was so long back. As he walked up to the grave, he thought the headstone should have something more written on it, not just the names and dates. There should be a descriptive sentence. Sean Coyne, murdered by his own bees. Jennifer Coyne, who died after a break-in at her home.

It was another mild day, unlike the day she was buried three years previously. Coyne remembered the rain. The relatives. The priest speaking a few words.

Busy place, a cemetery. Even in the short time it took Coyne to seek out the grave of his own parents and stand there to reflect a few minutes, at least five other funerals had taken place. People in Dublin were dying all the time. Every day. At all hours. Coyne heard the familiar sound of prayers coming across the gravestones but couldn't see the mourners until he moved a little and saw them huddled together, heads down, mostly in black.

Our Father who art in heaven . . . Somehow, the sound of another funeral was so much more vivid. The gash of an open grave, the raw look of wreaths and the fearful smell of flowers.

As Coyne started making his way back along the path, he almost ran straight into the man he had been trying to avoid for weeks. Mr Killmurphy. Killjoy, for Christsake, the man for all seasons now appeared to be hanging around the graveyard waiting for him. He was standing with his hands folded in prayer, pretending to be grieving. Coyne walked past him with his head down, but Mr Killmurphy turned around and spoke up in a calm voice.

Pat, he said. Pat Coyne.

Coyne's first reaction was to walk on. Ignore the bastard at all costs. But Coyne softened almost instantly when he saw the name of Nora Killmurphy on a gravestone. She had been dead all the time while Coyne was making his abusive phone calls. Jesus, Coyne should have known this. She never answered the phone.

Coyne stopped. The sound of a decade of the rosary on the breeze behind him.

Mr Killmurphy, he said.

I saw you in the shopping centre a few times, Pat. How are you these days?

Killjoy stepped forward and shook hands. Coyne found himself talking to his enemy: the man who had made his life hell and the man he had victimized for years in return; the man he would never forgive. Coyne looked at the gravestone and felt instantly sorry for him. He was overwhelmed with remorse and saw everything from Killjoy's perspective for the first time.

She died of cancer four years ago, Killjoy said, with his head down.

I'm sorry to hear that, Coyne said.

They exchanged some words of encouragement and Coyne ended up reciprocating with his own grief.

My mother, he said. Three years ago.

Killjoy said something stoical about life having to go on. He was always one for the daft and ceremonious, looking for some kind of financial parable to spout at you across his desk. And he was still wearing those pink shirts. But you couldn't be hard on a man in his grief, and Coyne's heart went out to him. Jesus, he was close to bursting into tears. Any minute he would be begging Killjoy for forgiveness. Please forgive me for damaging your property. Forgive me for the patio stuff, and all the phone calls.

I retired early to look after her, Killjoy said.

Coyne felt helpless. Tried to remember some of the anger that had sent him up to sabotage Killjoy's house that time. Killjoy had it coming! But it was all so far in the past now and he was unable to stop himself becoming Killjoy's friend. Here in the graveyard. United in mourning.

Coyne slowly opened up, baring his soul to Killjoy as though the cemetery had brought out some deep conciliatory unction. He explained how he'd been injured in a fire. How he was out of the Gardai now. And separated.

You always seemed like a perfect couple to me, Killmurphy said. I never would have thought . . . I'm sorry, you know, about all that trouble in the bank. I wish I could have been more generous.

Ah, no, Coyne said. You did your duty, Mr Killmurphy.

No, Pat. It's not good enough. I should have given you a break. It was wrong to call in the debt on a young couple like yourselves. I should have rescheduled. I should have written it off, in fact.

The conversion in the graveyard.

To hell with the bank, Killjoy kept saying. To hell with all their money. I should have been more generous.

No, Coyne insisted. It's me who should be apologizing. I'm sorry about all the trouble I caused. You know, all that damage, like.

Will you go away out of that, Killjoy said. You were a customer. You should have been treated better.

There was no need for the damage, Coyne said. And the phone calls. That was wrong.

What damage? Killjoy smiled. What are you talking about? Then he came around and slapped Coyne on the back. Told him not to mention it. His behaviour had been exemplary in the circumstances.

The truth lay hidden. It was clear that Killjoy had not made the connection. Coyne had come right out and admitted everything and Killjoy still didn't get it. He had no idea that Coyne was a terrorist. Perhaps some time in his sleep the whole thing would click and Killjoy's suburban arithmetic would finally reveal the formula. Coyne didn't have the heart to drag it all up again. I mean, that would have been worse than the original crime. Jesus that would kill him, to tell him now, at this late stage.

They walked away towards the gates together.

It was nice to meet you again, Killjoy said. Always like to keep in touch with my old customers. He even told Coyne to look him up in the telephone directory: perhaps they could go for coffee some day, now that they both had so much time on their hands.

Mongi O Doherty was not idly standing by. He was not the type to sit on his arse, *pro bono publico*, waiting for Sergeant Corrigan to come and point the finger at him. He was on the move, pursuing his own ambitions, looking at ways of recouping his losses, still hoping to extract the capital repayment from Jimmy Coyne. A pound of flesh if he couldn't actually get it in liquid currency.

The problem was that Jimmy Coyne had disappeared off the face of the earth, leaving no trace, not even with his family or friends.

Early afternoon, Mongi decided to call on Carmel Coyne to see if she could help. Stood on the threshold of the family home with his hoof in the door.

I'm looking for Jimmy, he said brusquely. He was getting desperate now, and there was no point in trying to pretend he was a friend or a Garda. No foil better than the blunt truth. Stare the mother in the eye and tell her you want to whack her son. Nothing more profoundly disturbing than that.

I don't know where he is, Carmel said, fiddling with the lock. Honestly.

The line was hard to sustain. It wasn't even worth saying, even if it was true. A mother who didn't know where her son was? And there was something even more dishonest about the way she tried to bang the door shut on Mongi O Doherty's footwear. As if she didn't notice the big pump-up runner stuck in her hallway.

Do you expect me to believe that, Carmel?

She was shocked to hear her own name. Then he stepped inside the house and produced a knife. Stood in the hallway and closed the door quietly, silent, solicitous, like a priest with bad news, looking her up and down and choosing his words carefully while his assistant went around the house searching the place for the money. Carmel could smell his smoky breath. The electrical hum of his nerves. He told her he was devoted to the physical force tradition – guns and blades, concrete blocks and glass shards, metal objects and syringes. He liked the sound of accidents and natural causes. He was particularly good on car crashes and was also the type to do most of his own creative dirty work. Held the knife up to her neck as though he was proffering it to her. Here, I'd like you to feel the edge on that. Sheffield steel – diamond sharpened.

You have no right to come in here! she shouted, all righteous and proprietorial. As if the whole thing was a matter of assertiveness. But the conviction had already left: she detected a kind of misfired irony in her own voice.

My husband is a Garda, she announced. He's due back any minute.

Oh, I see, Mongi said. He's not living in that flat any more?

Carmel had never felt so exposed. It was such a comprehensive defeat. Victim embarrassment. It was the lie, more than the attempted defence.

Leave us alone, she cried. Once again the plural, inclusive concept of the traditional family.

Look, don't start bawling like a fucking baby, Mongi shouted. He slapped her across the face and Carmel was suddenly left holding her burning cheek, blinking through tears, unable to cry. Didn't notice the trickle of blood flowing down her chin. She tried to swallow, but couldn't do that either.

The search of the house yielded nothing.

I'm going to clean this thing on your tits if you don't tell me where he is.

I swear, I don't know, Carmel whispered and then sank down. Collapsing in slow motion, trying to close over her light blue summer blouse.

He fucking owes me money! Mongi shouted.

He opened his mouth wide to pronounce the words. I'll be back, he said. Like news for the deaf. Then he prepared to make his point with a graphic illustration. Took Carmel's hand as though he was going to dance with her. Come dance with me, in Ireland!

Maybe it was some kind of parting handshake. Or more like a quick manicure. He pointed her index finger out and tucked the tip of the blade under the painted nail. Just one sharp little stab of dilated pain to drive his message home. Up through her arm and straight into the smarting tear ducts. By which time he had already stepped back and opened the door, pausing for a moment to look out before he disappeared. But as with all intruders, part of his persona still remained. Under the fingernails. As though he had only stepped out temporarily and would be back again any minute to continue. As though he was moving in. A new resident. Like a husband.

Coyne came across the poet with the four docile dogs outside the shopping centre. His face was very familiar from the Anchor Bar, but Coyne had never really had much to say to him. This time, in the street at the entrance to the town-killing shopping mall, there was something that attracted his attention. The poet had pinned a rough charcoal drawing of a man with a shaven head up on the wall behind him. Underneath was written the word 'Foe', in bold black letters. By induction, through the medium of verse, the poet was teaching his docile dogs to bite. Trying to turn these timid animals into selective killers. If they ever encountered this shaven-headed monster, alive or dead, they were instructed to turn instantly vicious.

Would you like a poem, sir?

But Coyne didn't see the point. I mean, everybody was spouting the stuff these days and nobody was listening. Poets vastly outnumbered readers. Coyne's advice was to change his career immediately. Offer himself as a listener. He'd make a fortune.

Coyne was more interested in the Identikit drawing. It was pinned up almost like a religious picture. Something to be venerated.

Who's that?

My enemy, the poet responded. Then he hunted through his portfolio for his best invective poems. Greatest hits of hate! Here, he said, and began reading out cantos of abuse and denigration, so that the dogs started growling at the drawing again. May you choke on a chicken bone. May you be thrown out in the rain. May you contract distemper and ringworm and the mange. Forsaken even by your own fleas. All the empirical suffering that dogs understood so well.

Coyne knelt down and examined the drawing. Finally interrupted the epic poem in order to extract some explanation for all this hatred. There was a time when every poet had a muse: some figure of great beauty that inspired him to place the chaos of the world behind him and seek perfection in words. Now they only had figures of great contempt. A poet could not work without a formidable enemy: some malicious bastard who had offended his honour and humiliated him. It made better source material. The poet as victim.

Coyne examined the drawing and became attracted to the notion of an anonymous, clearly defined but nameless adversary.

Can I buy it?

It'll cost you a fair whack, the poet said. Besides, what would I do? I'd be lost. I'd have to go back to writing love poems.

I'm offering you money for it, Coyne insisted.

Thou shalt not covet another man's enemy, the poet warned. You'd be taking your life in your hands. I'd feel responsible.

He was underestimating Coyne. There was no situation he was unable to handle. No enemy that he hadn't unceremoniously dispatched to the dustbin of history.

Except for himself. As enemies went, Coyne would never find anyone more formidable than himself. The battle with himself is the only one he would never win. The Identikit face seemed like a walkover. A skirmish. He haggled until the poet took the drawing down and handed it over, along with the strict advice that this man was armed and dangerous. Do not approach! The dogs snapped at the paper in Coyne's hand.

Slowly, Jimmy Coyne started changing his mind. The totality of his love affair with Irene Boland was under threat. He wanted to re-enter society and abandon the refuge of love in which he had become imprisoned like a captive.

I don't care if they kill me, he was now saying.

Don't go out there, Irene warned, trying to preserve the sanctuary of their relationship at all costs. Once Jimmy set foot outside, he would be murdered. It was like the archaic legend in which Jimmy would fall off his white horse and grow instantly old.

I'm going to renounce my wealth, he said.

In the long hours that he sat in the flat looking out to sea, he realized that he had been trapped into happiness. This was Jimmy's big re-think. What he now wanted was to be able to see both sides of the coin at once. Love and freedom at the same time. The great opposites.

He asked Irene to get the money. In the boiler room, he told her. Just reach into the back of the boiler and you'll find a bag. It's full of money, Irene, so be careful. I'd get it myself only I can't go in there any more.

What money is this? she asked.

Don't let anybody see you with it, Jimmy said, ignoring her enquiry.

Coyne was in the supermarket at the town-killing shopping centre when he was approached from behind by Irene Boland. He was standing close to the cornflakes. Jumped back in shock and smiled awkwardly.

It's about your son Jimmy, she said.

Where is he?

He remained non-judgmental. This woman standing in front of him like a store detective was almost Carmel's age. Jesus, she could be Jimmy's mother for Christsake. But Coyne could also see the attraction. The warmth in her eyes. The husky voice.

You've got to protect him, she said.

Why? What's wrong?

They're after him. They're gong to kill him.

Coyne pulled out the Identikit picture, right there in the supermarket with the sound of Frank Sinatra going his own way in the background and the voice of a woman breaking in telling them the price of chicken legs.

Is that him? Coyne asked.

I don't know, Irene said. I never saw any of them.

There were two women talking in one of the aisles not far away. One of them had a baby on her arm. She was listening to the other woman and rocking the supermarket trolley with her free hand. Back and forth, back and forth, making the groceries go to sleep. The hand that rocks the supermarket trolley.

I had to give him shelter, Irene Boland said. They attacked him and broke his ankle.

They'll hear from me, Coyne vowed. They better not lay a finger on him again or I'll kill them. He picked up a packet of Bran Flakes, realized he didn't normally buy that kind of thing and put it back.

They're after the money, Irene said.

What money?

Irene handed Coyne a bag full of dollars. Coyne opened it briefly and saw bundled notes inside.

They're the same people who killed the man at the harbour. Jimmy said that to me. He saw them.

Coyne looked all around him. At the meat counter there were some men in white coats and white hats that you could see the shape of their heads through. And matching red faces. On the wall was a gathering of these men smiling and standing around a table full of raw meat. Smiling at this slaughtered animal with their red spotty faces and white hats and canine eye teeth. Beside them another poster of a bull like a map dissected into territories. Cantons of rib roast and rump steak.

171

Where is Jimmy now? Coyne demanded. I need to speak to him.

No, she said.

There was something troubled about her: a kind of shakiness in the eyes. Then she turned and Coyne watched her walking away. She was small and plump and wore an ankle bracelet. He stood there with the bag of money, looking at the ankle bracelet under the tights. The red-faced butchers with their meat cleavers suspended in mid-air were joking and laughing among themselves.

Coyne went looking for Jimmy. Found out from the Haven nursing home where Irene Boland lived and stood ringing the bell early that evening. Irene not there at the time but Jimmy was looking out at his father below on the steps. He moved back from the window, but then sneaked forward again to watch Coyne ringing on bells next door and speaking to an old man for a moment. Once again he came back and rang on the right doorbell but got no answer.

Jimmy, frozen, held on to his fugitive status and allowed his father to knock and ring until he gave up and walked away, a vulnerable figure pacing away along the seafront in the closed cyberspace of his own thoughts.

That's my dad, he said to himself, and saw his own father for the first time with the brutal clarity of a curt description on a shampoo bottle – dry, damaged. A man with a limited vision. An absolutist. A sad bastard, carving a polite but determined path through a crowd of pedestrians who had come out for the evening with their children and their dogs and their buggies. His father was at odds with the languid mood of the evening, walking among the ordinary people of the city, locked in mortal combat with his phantasmal adversaries.

Jimmy felt sorry for him. It was unforgivable to ignore his own father like this. He changed his mind and decided to run after him. Wanted to re-enter his force-field of trust, perhaps walk out to the lighthouse together and talk about things the way they used to when Jimmy was still a child, convinced his father knew everything. Maybe hear some of the stories that were going on in Coyne's head and pretend that everything was all right again in the little republic of Coynes.

Mongi O Doherty had been awaiting this opportunity. It was inevitable that luck would fall his way at last, after so much scratching. It was like three identical numbers on a lottery card. He was there to intercept this emotional reunion between father and son. He and his assistant caught Jimmy crossing through the boat yard this time, asked him to sit in the back of the car and drove the short distance to the *Lolita* with a tape over his mouth to keep him quiet. Took him on board for a conference-style meeting, once the sun had gone down and the light was beginning to fade.

Jimmy was brought down below into the main cabin. There was an altercation with the skipper, Martin Davis who refused to allow his boat to be used as an interrogation centre. This is not Castlereagh. I can't have any inhuman and degrading treatment on my boat. He said he was finished with all of this stuff. He was going back to fishing.

I'm going clean, he said, but Mongi laughed out loud with his protruding teeth. What was clean about fishing? Besides, Martin Davis was in this business up to his neck. It was too late to get out now. So he agreed to take the *Lolita* for a spin around the bay. Started the engines and set off into the evening with the smell of diesel fumes all around.

They sat Jimmy down and pulled the tape off his mouth. Mongi sat down beside him and began to talk to him in a very polite tone.

Put yourself in my shoes, Mongi said. Don't you think I've been very patient?

Jimmy gave no response. Mongi's helper also remained quiet and the skipper was up on deck in the wheelhouse.

You're not listening, Mongi said, disappointed. I'm trying to enter into meaningful dialogue with you, for fucksake.

Hum! Jimmy looked up at Mongi. His ankle was beginning to swell up with referred pain. As though he was already suffering future injuries.

OK, let me give you an example, Mongi said. We've got plenty of time. I'll make it easy for you. What would you do if somebody robbed your dinner off you?

Jimmy looked helpless.

Just say you're in McDonald's, Mongi continued, and somebody comes up and swipes your Big Mac right off you. And it's your last money and you could be facing starvation. Snatches it out of your hand when you're just about to bite into it. How would you feel?

I don't know, Jimmy said. I hate McDonald's.

Abrakebabra then, or whatever?

That's worse.

OK. Bad example. What kind of grub do you like?

Italian.

Gimme a dish! Mongi clicked his fingers. Spaghetti or what?

Risotto.

Right, Mongi started once more, sitting back, not looking at Jimmy at all. You've got a bowl of risotto in front of you, and you stick your fork in. Then some fucking dickhead comes up and takes the fork off you, and the dish, and starts eating it up himself. And it's the last can of risotto left. What would you say?

I don't know, Jimmy said.

The boat was moving up and down on the swell. The engine was rumbling and sending deep vibrations through the boat: everything that wasn't fixed down was jumping with epileptic madness. Mongi's shoelace was swinging

rhythmically, doing a lasso imitation on its own. A key
hanging on a hook along the wall was dancing around in a
frenzy and a newspaper opened on the sports pages was
shivering.

Mongi sighed. I'm asking you a simple question, Jimmy. I
want you to dignify me with an answer. I bet you'd be a
little bit upset, wouldn't you?

I suppose.

I'm trying to do a quid pro quo with you, like. You're not
helping me.

I suppose I'd be upset all right.

Bloody right you would. You'd be fucking going apeshit,
man. Throwing a tantrum like a bawling baby. Mongi felt
he had been very understanding. He had acted like a
gentleman. That's what this is all about, Mongi said
philosophically. It's about taking food out of somebody
else's mouth.

Mongi decided to proceed to the amusements, as he
called them. We can do this the easy way or the hard way,
he said. If Jimmy told him where the money was, right now,
then they would go back in to the harbour and everything
would be cool. Mongi would be very lenient and let him off
with a battering. But if Jimmy did not make a full disclosure
straight away, Mongi would be forced to go the extra mile.
Jimmy thought of giving the money back, but it was too late
for that now. His father had it.

Amusements! Mongi shouted.

Coyne decided to walk along the pier. The anglers were
out, standing at the edge with their fishing rods, cigarettes
and sandwiches. At their feet, some stained newspapers
with live lugworm; one or two plaice already caught. From a
small radio a crackled and distant news-on-the-hour dis-
persed in the open air.

The pier was thronged with people. Some sat in the seats
by the wall – brown rust marks of bolts and metal supports

bleeding across the flaky blue wood like a crucifixion. The stigmata of seaside benches where people paused for a momentary review of life. Greatest moments. Worst disasters. End of century millennial self-analysis with the sunset over Dublin city leaving behind a sky of candy-floss streaks. Atomic dust particles turning the night over Dublin into a curtain of darkening pink and orange. The red glow on the granite rocks slowly faded and a white moon was already out on the far side of the wall, along with one or two bright stars. The wind gauge was not spinning like a propeller, for a change. Everything was calm. The Superferry slipped out with a moan of its siren echoing through the suburbs. And the lighthouse started casting an elliptical ring around the bay, whipping a long red finger across the black water, while the banjo player was playing the sad theme from *Doctor Zhivago*, warping the notes with added pathos.

Coyne saw the trawler making its way out through the harbour mouth but by the time he got to the top of the pier it was too far away to make out the name. The banjo player had moved on to other tunes – mazurkas, a waltz, ballads and polkas – all of which he covered in a blanket of trills and grace notes. Maybe it was all grace notes, in fact.

Coyne stood below the lighthouse and leaned against the wall facing out to sea. He was taking his time now. Things had become less rushed. Perhaps he should start letting things go a little more, become a tolerant man. A man without subtext. Perhaps he should do something useless. What a brilliant notion, he thought. It could be the great new catchphrase of our time: do something useless. There was far too much purpose in the world. It was all too productive and good and esteemed and valued. Why not something less viable.

Do something useless, he repeated out loud. He liked the sound of it.

He stared out to sea and listened to the music coming and going on the breeze. It was not quite summer yet and people were treating the good weather with great suspicion as usual. There was warmth left in the air, and a kind of afterglow in the rocks. As he leaned against the wall he felt it in his stomach, the latent heat of the sun stored in the granite. He was surprised by this sensation and it struck him almost like human warmth, pressing against his body. He had experienced nothing like it in such a long time. *Bolg le bolg!* Belly to belly! As though he was holding Carmel. Slow dancing with her to the music on the pier. The human warmth of the rocks.

Everybody was packed into the Anchor Bar that night when it opened its doors to the public again. Free pints for the first hour. All the familiar faces were there. Red-eye McCurtain was in early. And the poet. Free drink was all that mattered now.

The whole pub had been changed beyond recognition. There was no need for a snug any more. The curtains on the windows were also gone, allowing people to look right inside. It was an open society now. Nobody was hiding anything any more and the basic need for anonymity had gone. People wanted to be seen drinking. Young people sat in the window seats with bottles of foreign beer saying: Look at us, drinking and having fun. We are well-adjusted people, able to speak up for ourselves.

They had changed the name from the Anchor Bar to the Anchor Café. Gone too were the little partitions and the nautical artefacts. The interior architects had gone for transparency. Accountability! Generous open space and judiciously placed art objects. The Irish bar had evolved as a communal living room, allowing people to meet on neutral ground – a place of anonymity and fantasy. Now the Irish drinker was coming out at last. Spending more and drinking less.

Some of the local people were a bit put out by the price of the pint. Some complained about the music, said they couldn't hear themselves think. The poet was already lamenting the snug of Europe and said he was boycotting the pub, once the free beer ran out. The management was confident that the whole café idea would take off. There was an atmosphere of celebration and anyway they didn't give a shite whether they had a poet in the bar or not. Everybody was a poet as long as they had money.

The plaque to Tommy Nolan was unveiled quietly by Marlene Nolan. *I'm still rolling along* . . .

It was a Celtic disco pub. But already the little contradictions had crept back into the Anchor Café. Like the weekly golf tournament. And the weekly pub lottery. And the cliques and local gossip columnists. McCurtain had donated his *Playboy* calendar, which the barmen quickly pinned up on the side of the fridge door. Otherwise, it was a controlled environment, with a CD blasting out over the new sound system.

Martin Davis reluctantly steered the *Lolita* out into the Irish Sea. There was another altercation on board when the skipper told Mongi that he was meant to be in the Anchor Bar. He was meant to unveil a plaque.

Time for the amusements, Mongi said. Spectaculars!

Leave him alone, the skipper said from the wheelhouse. It's not worth it.

You do as you're told, Davis. Shut your jaw or I'll give you the mackerel.

Poll circe, the skipper muttered through his beard. If I woulda-hada-known there was this much violence involved, I woulda-never-hada-got into this.

Mongi had tied Jimmy to the railings on deck and had put him on a diet of stale fish. Just as he had done with the immigrants, he was shouting: Fresh fish! Despite the fact that Jimmy now had limp mackerel stuck in his oesophagus, coughing and gagging, with his eyes bulging out through his purple face, the force-feeding programme was not working any more.

It was counterproductive, Mongi decided. He took the mackerel out of Jimmy's mouth, like a stopper, and threw it to the seagulls. Then he lashed a long rope over the bow of the boat, working quietly in darkness with only the instrument panel lighting up the skipper's face in the wheelhouse and everybody's lips trembling with the shudder of the engine.

Did you ever see *Mutiny on the Bounty*? Mongi asked.

Martin Davis looked up. No, you can't do that, Mongi, he said.

Just a little dip. A little trip round the underworld.

Jesus, you'll kill him.

We'll be there on the other side when you come up, Mongi said to Jimmy. We'll be there to hear your confession.

But even as Mongi and his friend tied Jimmy's feet and hands and began to lower him down the side of the boat, with the utter darkness of the sea beneath him, Jimmy held fast to his ideals. Because that's all he had. He was blindly holding on to his faith. He could have given the money back. It would have been simple. But he went down into the inky black sea vowing to fight to the death. No Surrender.

Carmel had tried Coyne's flat once before that afternoon without success. Now she stood at the door again ringing the bell, with the engine of the car left running.

A man from the ground-floor flat came out and spoke to her. Coyne had not been in all day, as far as this man knew. So she decided to leave a note.

We need to talk, she wrote. Perhaps Coyne would read some subtext into this. So she wrote out a fresh note: Please contact me immediately regarding Jimmy. Then she posted the note through a crack under Coyne's door. Pushed it as far as she could with the pen, and left.

The darkness beneath the trawler made it seem like the underworld to Jimmy. There was darkness in his lungs too and he was coughing up an awful lot of water when he was pulled back up on deck again, retching grey spurts of brine and producing all kinds of sea debris. There was a cut over his eye. They sat him on a winch and gave him a minute to recover.

OK, Mongi said, slapping him on the back to help him breathe. Let me ask you one last time. If somebody took food away from you, what would you say?

Jimmy could not face the black water again and spoke up. Looked Mongi in the eye with great sincerity.

We're all in the vestibule, he said at last.

What's that?

You're in the vestibule, me and you.

Mongi turned his back on Jimmy in anger. His fists were balled as he looked towards the land and the string of lights along the coast. The sky above the city was reddish and inflamed.

You're making me do this, he said, turning back to face his victim.

They lifted him and brought him back to the side of the boat, Jimmy violently coughing up more in protest and the skipper standing by pleading with Mongi to stop. For Jesus sake, Mongi. He's not going to last.

He has a choice! Mongi shouted. It's not as though we didn't give him a chance.

Carmel walked straight into the Anchor Café amid all the celebration and commemoration. Just when Coyne was lifting up his pint and examining it at eye level in a moment of eucharistic admiration, she suddenly appeared, standing right behind him and calling out his name over the music. There was a worried look on her face, though she tried to smile back politely at all the local people who greeted her.

Great, Coyne thought. Jesus, things were looking up. If

this is what the café idea was intended to achieve, then he was all for it. More openness! More reconciliation! The only thing he regretted was that he didn't have a gin and tonic ready and waiting for her. The one day she decided to walk into the Anchor Café, he was not prepared.

I'm not staying, she said.

Ah, Carmel. Just have one, while you're here.

No way. She shook her head. And even when Coyne ordered a gin and tonic, she refused to touch it. We need to talk, she said.

Of course Coyne got it all wrong, thinking that she was trying to get back together with him at last. He was all flushed and emotional. He ran around looking for a barstool she could sit on.

Jesus, Carmel. I've been waiting for this moment.

What moment?

You know! Us, Coyne said. Us getting back together.

Jesus, Pat, she sighed. You've got this all wrong as usual. She quickly explained why she had come to the pub – the attack, the threat, the bandaged index finger. She hadn't come all the way down to the Anchor Café for her health.

Coyne was taken aback, not only by the blunt way in which she expressed her mind, but at the thought of her vulnerability. There was a little frown on her forehead that he had rarely seen before. He had always thought of her as being rock solid and could not imagine her unable to cope. Now he realized that she had come for help. She had not entered the Anchor Café of her own free will. She was calling on him as a protector of the home.

I should have gone straight to the police, she said.

I'll look after you, he said, still trying to salvage his pride.

It's Jimmy, she said. He's involved in something. This man says Jimmy owes him money. Big money.

I'm not a cop any more, Carmel, Coyne said at last, hurt. You're his father.

She said none of the things he would have expected to

hear. And could say nothing to reassure her. It was the wrong place for intimacy and Coyne was suddenly raging at the music. Called one of the barmen over and told him to switch it down. How could anyone talk while REM were howling and wailing their self-important, self-obsessed dirges all night? *Shiny, happy people holding hands!* For Jaysus sake!

Coyne and Carmel looked at each other, like they both agreed silently that this was a big disaster. There were things to be said but they were entirely out of context in this meeting. She was standing with her arms folded, a fortress of resentment and anger.

You're his father and you don't even know where he is, Carmel said, and then she started crying. With McCurtain looking on. And the poet. And the barmen. It was a true sign of transparency when customers in the new café began to show their feelings in public. Crying openly without shame.

Carmel turned and left. Coyne ran out after her and caught up with her just as she reached the car. He took the keys from her hand, opened the passenger door and ushered her inside. Got in and drove her home. Stopped short of the house and took out the Identikit drawing from his pocket.

Is this him? he asked.

Yes! How come? she said, looking up at Coyne as he stared out through the windscreen.

I'm going to look after this, he said, putting the drawing away again. Leave it to me.

Then he got out and brought her into the house. She was overwhelmed by the sudden conviction with which he assumed he could open the hall door, as in the old days, and lead her inside.

Everything will be OK, he said. I might need to use your car for a day or two.

He was a father again. He was the man of the house. Pat

and Carmel Coyne on the doorstep looking at each other for a moment through a blaze of confused emotion. He did something instinctive, something audacious that he would not have done if had thought about it. He threw his arms around her and gave her a hug: an awkward embrace that surprised him as much as it surprised her. It lasted only ten seconds and was over before they knew it. Before either of them could respond in words or work out what it was meant to signify. A gesture that was deep and lighthearted at the same time. It was over within seconds, but it lasted long enough for Coyne to feel the warmth of her body against his stomach, the latent heat of the sun, the slow dance with granite. The sensation that he had experienced on the pier earlier that evening. Human warmth.

Coyne drove back to his flat for the money. He left the engine running and ran inside to pick up the bag. On his way out he saw Carmel's stone on the mantelpiece and put it in his pocket. Then he bounded down the stairs and out to the car, only to find Sergeant Corrigan waiting for him.

Corrigan was always going to be one step behind, like a transmuting virus piggy-backing on small details of information. At times he tried to get one step ahead of the action, but he found himself shifting back as though he was dealing with a relativity principle in which he was contantly catching up with crime, his time-travelling twin brother. One day he would arrive before something happened.

Sergeant Corrigan stepped forward out of the shadows, whistling, just as Coyne was getting into the car. Where is he? Corrigan demanded.

Coyne looked around and saw two other officers sitting in an unmarked Garda car. They were so obvious. For Christsake. You give yourselves away. It's like you have a big sign on the roof of the car saying: We are watching you! What kind of surveillance is this, he thought, when you can spot them a mile off. Corrigan should have brought his hurling stick so he could whack the ball and his two greyhound colleagues could go and run after it.

Do you know the one about Achilles and the tortoise? Coyne asked.

What are you getting at?

You know, Achilles, the guy with the wings on his hat. The fastest man on two feet. Well he has this race with a tortoise and gives him a bit of a head start, on account of him being so slow, you follow me.

I'm warning you, Coyne. I've had about enough of this shite.

Hang on a second, Coyne said. You see this fella, Achilles, no matter how fast he is or what medals he's got for running, is never going to catch up. Because every time he catches up, the tortoise has moved on a fraction. And so on into infinity.

So! What's your point, Coyne?

Well, that's the way it is with the law. That's why I got out of the Gardai. No matter what you do, no matter how fast you can get your greyhound detectives there to run, you never catch up with crime, 'cause it's already moved on a little bit.

Look, Coyne. Would you mind stepping out of the car. I think we'll have to sort this out at the station.

Wait, Coyne said.

He took out the Identikit picture of Mongi O Doherty, gave it to Sergeant Corrigan and asked him to take a good look at the face.

That's the man you want, Coyne said.

Who's this? Corrigan demanded.

Mr X. He's the man you're after.

Then Coyne drove off, leaving Corrigan on the street staring at the drawing. Coyne turned the corner with a little too much fervour, giving another characteristic yelp of the tyres to wake up the neighbours. A statement of great hope, echoing around the canyons of suburbia while Sergeant

Corrigan looked up and beamed out at his colleagues with epiphenomenal satisfaction. He seemed to have made the big breakthrough at last. A confluence of evidence. As he folded up the tattered drawing of Mongi O Doherty, he felt everything was finally beginning to sit perfectly. As though the map of Ireland had been folded up incorrectly for years into an awkward bulging mess, cartography forced together in a strained and hasty arrangement. Now at last it was beginning to fit more snugly, collapsing effortlessly into the intended folds.

Coyne drove at great speed towards the harbour, full of renewed determination. He knew what had to be done. The war to end all wars. The final showdown.

Along the way, however, Coyne put his foot on the brake and brought the car to a halt with a howl that cut through the quiet streets, piercing through dreams and half-sleep. Rubber burning and a blue cloud rising from the tyres. It looked like he had suddenly remembered something and could go no further. The car was stopped dead in the middle of a side street. He opened the door, got out and stood for a moment, looking around and listening, struck by a vision. The street was empty. Most of the lights in the bedroom windows were out. The city was asleep.

Yes! He would start here. At Clarinda Park. This is where he would begin his modest enterprise. He had Carmel in mind now. Inspired by the granite warmth of her stomach. No question about it. He would start here.

Coyne opened the hatchback door, laid out a rug along the boot and went off searching in the gardens. It wasn't long before he came across the first rocks. Grey boulders like dinosaur eggs lined up along the path. He lifted the first of them and brought it over to the car, placed it in the boot and looked at it with satisfaction before going back for the next one. With the engine running all the time, crooning the neighbourhood back to sleep, he worked away quietly, lifting the rocks one by one and putting them in the boot of the car. Each time he stopped for a brief moment to stand back and look at the progress of his work. When the boot was full, he put some more on the back seat. Already, there was a sense of industry about all of this. Coyne was becoming efficient. And when the car could take no more, he drove away, listing to one side as he dragged along the road up the hill. He could hear the moan of the suspension as it laboured in second gear all the way.

He had chosen a place already, long ago on one of his walks. Like any visionary, he had seen the end result in front of his eyes many times. All that remained now was the execution – the physical birth of the idea.

He was doing something useless at last. Something less viable. Something gloriously unproductive and unacclaimed.

He parked the car as close as he could and began to carry the rocks up to the nearest seaward point of the hill, a promontory high up overlooking Dublin Bay. It was deserted there at night, and he found he could easily work by the light of the moon. There was a metallic sheen across the bay too and the night was now almost as bright as day. One by one, he carried these boulders quietly, heaving them out of the car and lumbering all the way up the hill, then stopping briefly to look at the bay surrounded by its necklace of yellow lights out to Howth. He was sweating now and breathing heavily. It seemed to him that his rasping breath could be heard all over the city as he worked. Now and again he took out his inhaler and had a quick blast before going back to work. He never looked at his watch once.

When this consignment of rocks had all been delivered to the site, he drove back down into the suburbs looking for more. Got a large bottle of water at one of the chippers and stood there drinking it while other people walked away with chips. He went back to work immediately, tiptoeing through people's front gardens and taking their precious rocks from under their eyes without as much as the sound of a footfall or a cough. It was a stunning crime, one that nobody would be able to explain the following morning. A local mystery. Why would anybody steal rocks that were free in the first place? It was an incomprehensible assault on the idea of suburbia.

Coyne dragged the next load up through the back streets towards his site. Worked again like a labourer with unlimited endurance until the stones were delivered to this strange construction site. This would be a decent monument, he thought to himself as he sat back and drank more water. This is one that will mystify them all, an overnight monument erected by the spirits. Underneath would be a bag full of dollars that nobody in the world knew about except Coyne.

As he worked, all kinds of random images floated into his consciousness. Pleasant thoughts of when his children were small and he used to let them jump off tables and cupboards into his arms. He remembered some of the stories he used to tell them. In particular the one about the woman with the silver voice. He stopped to think of that one. The woman had such an exceptional voice, such a beautiful and powerful voice that she placed the whole country under a spell. Everybody was compelled to listen to it. People in cars stopped at the side of the road. People on the streets of Dublin stopped to catch her voice emerging from a radio through open windows of upper rooms. Even robbers trying to break into a house would have to drop everything. A curfew reigned over the whole country while she sang, so that even if there was a war on, they would have to stop. Years later, the children still half believed it. He half believed it himself as he went back to work and started building his foundations.

Out on the bay, Mongi was preparing to send Jimmy down

to the black waters for the last time. He gave his victim one last chance, but Jimmy had no way of saving himself now. In the end it was the skipper, Martin Davis who came to his rescue. This was going too far. He was already crippled with remorse over the death of Tommy Nolan and was not willing to face another one. He stepped into the wheelhouse and got the flare gun. Shot the bright red star into the sky, turning their faces pink and turning the water all around them into a wine-coloured bath as it dropped down over the sea.

Mongi looked up. He shouted at the skipper and ran to the bridge, trying to restrain him from firing another shot. There was a fierce scuffle but it was of no consequence. The lifeboat was already on its way out of the harbour towards them.

Coyne saw the activity in the bay. He looked up and saw the flare shooting into the sky, arching down over the sea like a red comet. He noticed the lifeboat heading out towards the furthest point, close to the horizon. It was such a clear night that he could see the white parting of foam on the side of the boat as it rode the swell. Down in the town there was more activity. Blue lights of Garda cars and ambulances at the harbour, sirens whooping through the main street.

Coyne was locked into his work. He grafted right through the night, not feeling the slightest fatigue. At one point he placed the stone with the Saturn ring down into a neat gap in the foundations. Back in the town collecting more rocks, he saw a figure coming towards him along the street with a dog. He thought he was caught now surely: one of the neighbours coming to investigate. Soon they would call the Guards. But then he saw that the person was accompanied at a distance by various dogs. Four dogs, he counted. Just as Coyne was having trouble with an extra-large boulder, the dreadlock poet came on the scene and started asking what he was up to.

It's a folly, Coyne explained.

The poet watched Coyne struggling with the rock and saw the great determination in his face. A folly, he said. You mean, like in the famine times.

Yes, Coyne said.

The poet gasped with admiration. He wanted to belong to this. He liked it. The great unacclaimed, non-functional, existential beauty of it. His entire body of work had been marked by obscurity. He was emotionally and artistically close to all things unremarkable and unnoticed.

He offered to help and Coyne agreed to bring him along up the hill after first swearing him to secrecy. It was important that nobody ever found out who constructed this folly. They talked about dry stone walls for a while and the poet was good at selecting the right kind of stones. Along the way, they came across a mound of granite rocks which would do perfectly for the outer shell. Nor was the poet averse to physical endeavour.

The work was beginning to accelerate. All through the night this pair of labourers worked diligently, with very little talk between them, except for a moment here and there when the poet thought of something and said it out loud to commit it to memory. The dogs sat close by, one of them looking out to sea and the others curled up asleep, or just keeping an eye on the work. At one point, the poet stopped to ask Coyne a question.

What did you do with the enemy?

I gave him away, Coyne said.

Pity, the poet said. You don't often come across enemies as good as that.

Maybe he never existed at all, Coyne said.

Maybe Ireland never existed, the poet laughed.

Perhaps he was right, Coyne thought. Maybe Ireland was not a real place at all but a country that existed only in the imagination. In the songs of emigrants. In the way people

189

looked back from faraway places like Boston and Springfield, Massachusetts. Maybe it was just an aspiration. A place where stones and rocks had names and stories. Maybe this was the glorious end. The end of Ireland.

By the time they finished building the cairn, the light was coming up over the horizon, seeping along the coast from Wexford. A nascent brightness edging the sky closer and closer to blue. From where they stood beside the overnight monument they could see the shape of the world and the texture of the water: choppy, like elephant hide at that distance. Slowly the colours were emerging. Around them, the grass turned green and the hedges took on a dark blue. And the shapes of the rocks became clear, so that Coyne could now see the individual shade of each rock they had used. Now he could appreciate the full effect of his achievement.

Up above them the seagulls were on the move, flying from right to left as they did every morning at that time. Flying silently with the same determination with which he and the poet had worked all night on his construction. The birds seemed to have somewhere specific in mind as they flew across the bay from Wickow or Arklow up to Dublin and on past Howth and Lambay Island. Silently. Many of them in small V-shaped formations with leaders and followers; others just going it alone. The great exodus of dawn. Not stopping for anything. Not remotely interested in food or in anything on the surface of the sea. They were crossing the bay at a great altitude, like vectors all going in the same direction across a screen. Hundreds of them emerging with the light in the south and flying with great self-knowledge towards the north.

Coyne went to the hospital the following morning to see Jimmy: sitting up in bed with a blue tube across his nostrils, he looked pale and serene. Beside him the usual bottle of Lucozade and some grapes that Irene Boland had brought in before she went to work. Coyne was completely over-whelmed by events and only slowly began to emerge from his obsession with the cairn when he met Sergeant Corrigan in the corridor.

He's co-operating, Corrigan smiled. A vital witness for the state.

Jimmy had become an overnight hero. Martin Davis was there too, anxiously hoping to hear how the young lad was doing. And Sergeant Corrigan was clapping Coyne on the back, thanking him for the Identikit picture.

I know what you're going to say, Jimmy whispered as Coyne entered the room and stood beside the bed looking at him.

No, Coyne said. As a matter of fact, I wasn't going to say anything.

The vestibule!

Coyne put his hand on Jimmy's shoulder. Things had shot ahead beyond his control. It seemed he had only briefly controlled anything in his life once or twice when the children were very small. He listened quietly now as Jimmy talked.

When Carmel came into the room some time later there was more silence. It looked like the big reunion in many ways – Coyne and Carmel back together again in the hospital, sitting on either side of Jimmy's bed. Carmel holding Jimmy's hand. Coyne unshaven and exhausted, waiting for her to say something, to make a move, perhaps to hold his hand as well as Jimmy's. He thought of showing her what he had built. But the cairn remained undiscovered. He kept it to himself.

Coyne picked up one of the grapes in the basket and put it in his mouth. Carmel looked at him as he crunched on the seeds.

Have you had breakfast yet, he asked her.

No, she said.

Do you fancy a rasher?

Ms Dunford had arranged everything. She had contacted the school and set up the whole thing with the principal. Psycho-drama. Ms Dunford would write books on the subject one day. Coyne's uncharted emotions, like discovering America.

Some weeks later she collected him at his flat, smiling at him with her bottom row of teeth as he came out the front door. She was dressed up for the occasion. Perhaps a little too much make-up for Coyne's liking; it looked like her face was already beginning to crack into little lines at the side of her eyes. But she was very happy. And quietly excited by the fact that Coyne had finally agreed to this visit.

They drove towards the city on a warm morning in mid-June. The school was still open and there were a few days left before the summer holidays. There was no pressure on Coyne to do this, she explained once more in the car. He was doing nothing against his will. And he understood that he could pull out of this at any moment if it made him uneasy. Ms Dunford kept talking all the time while Coyne remained silent. Anxious.

The familiarity of the school surprised him; nothing had changed since he was a boy. The ancient stuffed bird display in the glass case outside the principal's office. The shiny banisters. Echoes of children floating through the stairwell and the smell of chalk and dusters as Coyne was ushered into the classroom like a school inspector from the Department of Education. *Rang a Ceathar – Cailíní!* The girls turned and looked at him with awe and curiosity, perhaps also with some amusement as he smiled awkwardly and tried to fit into one of the benches at the back of the class with his big clumsy knees. He compromised by sitting sideways in the end. He listened to the teacher resume her geography class, all about the Nile. Now and again, one or two of the girls still looked around at him furtively. But he was lost in a slide of sense memory, sifting through a gallery of mental possessions. He could remember his mother wearing a summer hat and a blue polkadot dress as she collected him from school. He remembered a plastic water-squirting camera on his first Holy Communion. And there was a familiar sensation at the back of his throat, like the sweet and slightly nauseating taste of custard.

It was lunchtime when he got around to the boys' section. A hastily built blockwork extension, never plastered. He remembered the familiar grey, tin wastepaper bins. And there was nothing quite like the silence left behind in an empty classroom, with the collective voices of boys and girls coming in from the yard outside. It induced a kind of dreamy surrender as he wandered around the abandoned desks. He read a sentence in the Irish language on the blackboard. Found his own former desk and examined a copybook lying open on it. Remembered the opening lines of a poem he once learned off by heart about a hanging in Ballinrobe.

Out in the yard, as he walked into the full volume of children's voices, he thought of the sandwiches falling out of Tommy Nolan's hand. He stood at the spot where it happened, but was distracted by the sight of two small girls talking to each other and eating their lunch. No more than five years old, they were oblivious to the noise and action around them. One of them was trying to pull the hair away from her eyes, and her mouth. She held her white bread sandwich up in her hand and Coyne could see the shape her bite had left behind. Like a little ticket-machine bite. A small, neat semicircle. A perfect crescent.